Sophia Cobbs'
WONDROUS WORLD
OF WITCHCRAFT

Double
Trouble

SOPHIA COBBS

SilverWood

Published in 2023 by SilverWood Books

SilverWood Books Ltd
14 Small Street, Bristol, BS1 1DE, United Kingdom
www.silverwoodbooks.co.uk

ISBN 978-1-80042-264-3 (paperback)
Also available as an ebook

British Library Cataloguing in Publication Data
A CIP catalogue record for this book
is available from the British Library

Page design and typesetting by SilverWood Books

SOPHIA COBBS was born in 1982 in Dendermonde, Belgium. She has always had a fondness for writing. In high school she wrote poems and short stories but mostly kept them to herself.

This is her second novel.

Besides a vivid imagination she also has some theatrical drama in her life: she is a theatre director and actress, currently practicing in Ghent, Belgium, where she lives.

When she isn't writing or directing, she is doing one of two things: working for her own company where she gives administrative advice to small companies or scouring wine tastings with her husband.

Also by Sophia Cobbs

Sophia Cobbs' Wondrous World of Witchcraft and Misery

I dedicate this book to my husband, Wim, for putting up with all my quirks and being so supportive about all my ideas and projects. Thank you.

One

The Meet Cute

The sun was shining. There were only a few clouds in the sky. A couple of birds were singing and tumbling over each other. It was the last days of spring.

Miss Level raised her pinkie in the air and held it still for a few seconds. "Two more days and summer begins." She put her hand down. "And not a moment sooner." She smiled and bent down to pick up her basket. She was picking herbs so that she could make a nice cup of tea when she got back to her cottage.

Suddenly, she felt uneasy. She wasn't quite sure what had just happened. Looking around, she cautiously started walking back to her cottage. She picked up the pace a little, still glancing left and right.

Then something smacked into her and she fell back on her butt.

"Hey!"

A scared-looking woman was sitting on the ground right in front of her. "I am sorry." The woman glanced behind her as she tried to get up.

Miss Level peered into the woods. "What are you looking for?"

"Nothing," the woman replied, looking right at her. She straightened and reached her hand down. "Let me help you."

Miss Level smiled and accepted the proffered hand. The moment she was back upright, she looked the woman up and down. She didn't seem to be dangerous or anything, but she did seem scared. Miss Level was also quite certain that this woman was a witch.

As she was still holding the woman's hand, she shook it. "I am Miss Level. Who are you?"

The woman blinked at her. "Euh, Petulia." She tried to get her hand back. "My name is Petulia."

"Nice to meet you," Miss Level replied, just before releasing her hand. "Well, you look like you could use a cup of tea."

"I don't think—" Petulia started.

"Oh, don't worry." Miss Level flapped her hands. "Whatever you were running from, it isn't chasing you." She bent down, shoved the spilled herbs back into her basket, and stood up again. "Now," – she turned to Petulia – "let us go to my cottage and you can tell me all about it." She turned away from the woman, certain that she would follow. "I did feel a weird vibe in the air just before you crashed into me but I couldn't quite make out what it was."

Petulia stared after the small figure who continued to talk as she walked away from her. A little confused, she started to follow. One more glance over her shoulder revealed…nothing.

Two

Sticks and Stinking Stew

To be honest, to the untrained eye, it looks like a stick; just a little, crooked twig with nothing special about it, lying on Hickory Street in Wakefield, Kansas. So people just pass it by. But when Tobias Thomson kicks it – just because he is in a sulky mood – it shoots up, performs a beautiful somersault, and lands perfectly on the concrete before dropping gracefully onto its side.

That, however, is not what catches Tobias's attention. It has a certain glow. Not a reflection of the light on its wet bark or something like that. No – it's something dark that seems to come from the inside. It is almost like it absorbs all the surrounding light, creating a small but stark contrast with everything else. So, Tobias picks up the stick. As soon as his fingers touch the wood, he feels an enormous amount of energy flowing through him.

"What the…" He just looks at it. Curious, he turns it around and around in his hand. The dark glow seems to intensify, so he starts twirling it. Then, on a whim, he flips it into the air, where it creates a hole which grows larger and larger until a dark, human-sized portal appears. Being the adventurous type, Tobias just steps through it. Right before he vanishes completely, he grabs the twig and takes it with him.

The portal closes abruptly. Suddenly, he finds himself on a hot desert plain. The sun is scorching. Tobias immediately takes off the red sweater he is wearing and lets out a foul curse.

"Great. This looks like fun." Sarcasm is his default setting. He looks around and sees nothing but sand. Wiping some sweat from his brow, he notices that he still has the twig in his hand. "I wonder..." He starts spinning the twig again and, just like before, another portal opens up.

This time, he ends up in a beautiful forest, full of life. The trees are covered with leaves. The colour of them is an almost unbelievable green. A couple of birds fly up from one of the branches and dance through the air. A squirrel runs up a trunk, stops, and stares at Tobias before deciding that he isn't an interesting enough subject and climbing further up the tree. Tobias looks around in amazement and wonders where he has ended up, only to decide that it doesn't really matter, does it? Smiling, he starts walking.

About half an hour later, he walks out of the forest and comes to a meadow. A fence surrounds it but there is nothing in it except grass and a few very big piles of earth that he assumes were made by moles. He decides to risk it and jumps the fence. As he walks through the meadow, he notices a small gate on the other side. He might as well, so he changes his direction slightly in a westerly direction and walks on.

Had he gone straight ahead and jumped the fence again, he would have come to a crossroads, walked straight on, and eventually ended up in Clariceville. Now, the only choice he has is left or right. He chooses left, which, unfortunately for Tobias, will not bring him anywhere near a village, town or city for quite some time.

In the forest Tobias just walked through, there is an honest-to-God gingerbread house, which is home to two witches and one man with horns. Lately, the tension between the witches in this cottage has been growing exponentially, and today is the day when it will come to an abrupt end.

"I can't see what the problem is." Miss Level looks around the kitchen. Every nook and cranny is clean. There aren't any dirty dishes or other things lying around.

"No, you can't, can you?" Petulia is standing next to the sink with her hands on her hips, staring at Miss Level.

"Well, explain it, then."

"He made blueberry pancakes!" Petulia's voice rises, causing a few birds outside to fly away and look for cover.

Miss Level still doesn't understand. "You like his pancakes. You ate six of them."

"That's not the point!"

"Then what is?" Miss Level is usually a very calm person, but Petulia is really pushing it.

"He cleaned up!" Petulia waves her hands around the spotless kitchen.

Miss Level just stares at her. "You're mad because he cleaned up?"

Petulia suddenly realises that this is indeed a bit peculiar but she isn't going to give in now. She lifts her chin and haughtily replies, "That is *my* job."

"Fine. I will tell him never to clean up in this house again." With those words, Miss Level turns around and walks away from Petulia, thinking that her best friend might have just completely lost her mind.

Petulia turns back to the sink and grabs the dishcloth. She wipes down the already perfectly clean table, all the while mumbling that she will not be made redundant in her own home.

Miss Level enters her bedroom and finds the man she adores in bed, leafing through *The Clarice Times*. As she climbs into bed, he drops the newspaper and raises one perfect eyebrow. Of course, he heard something going on downstairs but wisely decided to stay in the bedroom.

"I am to tell you not to clean anything any more. Apparently, that is Petulia's job."

Gabriel just shrugs and opens the paper again.

"Are there any new listings in there? Houses for sale?" Miss Level doesn't want to leave but Petulia is making life very difficult. Every day, there's always something Gabriel has done wrong. Well, not really *wrong*; just wrong in Petulia's mind. Who gets angry because someone else cleans the kitchen? Most people would just be thrilled that they didn't have to do it. Miss Level is. She gives a sigh and rests her head on Gabriel's shoulder.

They both look at the listings in the paper until they suddenly notice a small advertisement at the bottom of the page: 'Small cottage, recently renovated, for sale. Furniture included.'

"That would be perfect," Miss Level says. "I will call them tomorrow, see if we can take a look at it."

Gabriel just nods, smiles, and kisses the top of her head before they both go to sleep.

Tobias has been walking for a while now and is starting to get hungry. An hour ago, he began to look around for an inn or something – anything, really – so that he could eat and rest. No such luck. Very tired now, he sits down at the foot of a big oak tree.

He could, of course, try to open up another portal, but what if he ends up in the desert again? He will be worse off. Besides, he likes this place. It's very green and the air is fresh. Just to prove it, he inhales deeply, and immediately yawns.

Maybe the stick can do more than just open portals. He lifts the stick and looks at it. Even if it can do more, how can he get it to do whatever it can do? He already knows that twirling it opens portals. Maybe if he swishes it? Nothing. Maybe he needs to say something. "Abracadabra." Swish. Nothing. He points the stick at a nearby tree. "Abracadabra." Again, nothing.

Suddenly, he realises he is being ridiculous. He should probably think about something he wants before swishing and pointing all over the place. He points the stick at the same tree, closes his eyes and focuses. "Food." Opening one eye, he glances at the tree, but nothing edible is waiting for him. He squeezes his eyes shut and tries again. "Please, just anything. Right now, I'll even settle for my mom's stinking stew."

Of course, this is the moment when the stick complies with his request. When Tobias opens his eyes again, a bowl of steaming stew is sitting at the foot of the tree. Too hungry to care, he jumps up, runs to it, drops to his knees and wolfs everything down. It's only afterwards that he realises that it was indeed his mother's stew. The aftertaste really lingers...

Satisfied that he has eaten something, he tries to conjure up a tent. But it is only when he thinks about the ugly orange tent that belongs to his younger brother that the stick works. Now, Tobias isn't the dumbest person in the world, so he quickly realises what he must do to get things done when working with the stick. As he starts to unpack the tent, he makes a mental note to only think about new, shiny things in the future.

Three

Ripples in the Sky

The next morning, Miss Level finds Petulia sitting at the kitchen table.

"You're up early."

"Yes. I don't know why, though." Petulia frowns. "Why are *you* up?"

Miss Level fills the kettle with water and puts it on the stove. She opens a cupboard, pulls out the box filled with different kinds of tea, and puts it on the table. After that, she takes two cups, closes the cupboard and sits down next to Petulia. "I don't know either. I got this funny feeling last night and didn't sleep at all. Like something is messing up the balance."

They sit silently next to each other until the kettle starts to whistle. Miss Level takes it off the stove while Petulia opens the box of tea and chooses Earl Grey for herself and camomile for her friend.

As they wait for their tea to steep, they look out the window. And a good thing too; otherwise they would have completely missed the ripple in the sky.

"Did you see that?"

"Of course I did." Petulia is already getting up and walking towards the coat rack. "Are you coming?"

Miss Level looks down at her dressing gown. "I'm not really dressed for it. Give me ten minutes." She quickly gets up and runs up the stairs.

While Miss Level is getting ready, Gabriel comes downstairs, already fully dressed.

Before he can do or sing anything, Petulia says, "You can't come with us."

Gabriel just frowns.

"It's a magic thing so you will just get in the way. Besides, somebody has to watch the house." She crosses her arms in front of her chest, daring him to argue.

He doesn't. He just shrugs and walks over to the stove to fill a cup of his own with tea and water, thinking that he probably doesn't want to be near her anyway when Miss Level gives her the news.

It annoys Petulia that she doesn't get any response out of him, so she turns, grabs her coat and walks out the front door.

Miss Level rushes downstairs and is surprised to not find Petulia standing there, hands on her hips, tapping her foot. She looks at Gabriel, who only points to the front door in response.

She smiles, quickly kisses him, and puts on her coat. "I'm sure we won't be too long. We will probably be back before dinner." And then she rushes out the door, only to bump immediately into Petulia, who is standing just outside. As a result, Petulia and Miss Level both fall. Miss Level smiles apologetically. "Sorry."

Petulia stands up and brushes the dirt off her coat. While her friend starts to do the same, she is already looking up at the sky to see if any new ripples have appeared. None. "We should go west. I think it came from there."

Miss Level, who doesn't really know which way west is, just nods and waits for Petulia to lead the way.

As per usual, Petulia has no problem whatsoever with assuming the role of leader. To be completely honest, lately she has missed it. That is probably the reason why she picks so many fights with her friend, but she will never admit it. If Miss Level doesn't understand that, then so be it. She quickly starts walking to escape those pesky thoughts.

Miss Level is hoping that this little trip will ease her friend's mind and lift her foul mood. The moment that happens, she will let her know that she and Gabriel are moving out, even though the house is actually hers. Now does not seem to be the right moment.

As you might have guessed already, the ripple in the sky was caused by Tobias. He, of course, has no idea that it happened because, let's be honest, he is new to the whole magic scene. When he woke up this morning he was hungry again, so he thought really hard about scrambled eggs, bacon, toast, fresh orange juice, and coffee. The stick did the rest. But it also created the ripple in the sky that was noticed by several people, including Petulia and Miss Level.

While Tobias eats his breakfast, he thinks about what he is going to do afterwards. Usually, he doesn't really think things through before doing them. Proof of that came yesterday: a portal opened up and, without any thought about it, he just stepped through it. The first time wasn't a big success, but this place seems nice. The only problem is, he has no idea where he is or where he is going. Yesterday, he didn't notice any buildings along this road, and he is beginning to wonder if he has taken the right route. It would be so much easier if he had an idea of where he was.

Suddenly, he grabs the stick, points it, and thinks really hard about a map of some sort. He opens his eyes to find a scroll at his feet. Cleaning his hands on his shirt, he picks it up. Partially unfurling the parchment, he can see part of a painted forest with a path running through it. This might be helpful. But first he is going to finish his breakfast, and then he will check the whole map and see if he can find his exact location.

As he continues to eat his eggs, he realises the tent is still standing there. He isn't going to carry the damn thing, so he points the stick, and it vanishes. Tobias doesn't really think about where it has vanished to. He just wants it gone and it is. The ripple that shoots up into the sky once more still goes unnoticed by him.

He cleans his hands on his shirt again and opens out the entire parchment. It is about thirty centimetres high and forty centimetres long. There is indeed a forest painted on it; more specifically, the forest he is in. He can see the path he took yesterday, and notices a red spot right in the middle of the map. Is that where he is right now? How peculiar. Unfortunately, he can't find any buildings on the map, so he must decide whether he will continue his journey or go back to where he came from.

Just at that moment, a small leaf falls onto the map. As Tobias brushes it away, the map moves. Or rather, the parchment itself doesn't move at all, but the forest painted on it shifts a little to the right. Even the red spot is now three centimetres to the right of where it was before. This is very interesting. Tobias immediately starts swiping the picture from left to right, up and down, until he can see a town in the top left-hand corner. The red spot is now all the way down in the bottom right corner, but at least he is still on the map, right?

Decided, he stands up with the parchment still unfurled in his hands and walks a little to the west. The red spot on the map moves the tiniest bit in the correct direction. He smiles and rolls up the parchment. Putting it in his back pocket, he continues walking, leaving the remnants of his breakfast behind.

Deep in the forest, he awakes. He inhales deeply and smiles.

"Raw power. Undisguised. Mine for the taking."

He opens his eyes. Still trapped in this damn tree, but it doesn't matter. If whoever it is keeps sending out ripples of magic with no purpose, he can seize them and be free soon enough. And then...

Oh, the world isn't ready for that. If they thought he was bad before, he will be the Devil incarnate this time.

"Damn it." Petulia starts walking a lot faster. "Whoever it is should really pay closer attention to what they are doing."

Miss Level hurries to keep up with her friend, but having shorter legs is not helping. "You are right. I have a bad feeling about this."

"At least we know we are going the right way." Petulia turns around briefly. "Hurry up, will you?"

"I'm going as fast as I can. You do remember that my legs are shorter than yours, don't you?"

Of course, Petulia realises that her friend is right, but she cannot slow down. She has a funny feeling that something evil is waiting. They just don't have the time to slow down. They need to stop whoever it is, and quickly. She glances over her shoulder. "We don't have much time. Just hurry."

Suddenly, Miss Level stops walking. She is panting and getting pains in her side. Bending over slightly, she says, "Please… stop for…just a minute…"

Petulia stops, standing with her hands on her hips. She too is slightly out of breath but refuses to show it. "Come on."

Miss Level holds up one hand. Her breath is calming somewhat. When she looks up at Petulia, her gaze slips past her and she starts to smile.

Petulia follows her gaze. Immediately she shakes her head. "No, no, no. Not again."

Miss Level walks past her and picks up the thick branches that have caught her eye. "You know as well as I do that this would really help to speed things up."

She hands one of the branches to Petulia, who reluctantly accepts it. "Just so you know, I protest."

"Of course, you do." Miss Level stands in front of her. "Go on. Up!"

Petulia raises her branch in her arms and holds it horizontally. Miss Level closes her eyes, also holding her branch horizontally, and starts mumbling. A faint purple glow spreads from her hands into the wood. Then a small spark hops from her branch to Petulia's, causing it to glow as well.

When Miss Level opens her eyes, both pieces of wood have transformed into solid purple brooms. "There! That ought to do it!" She sweeps her broom between her legs and sits down. Immediately, she starts to hover. "Well, go on."

Sulkily, Petulia follows her example. "Why always purple? We are witches, and very old ones at that. We shouldn't fly around on purple brooms. They should be old and dull, like us."

"Petulia, when have we ever been dull? Old, yes, but dull? Never!" And with those words, Miss Level laughs and flies off.

Grumbling, and a lot more unsteady, Petulia follows.

Four

Wally

Tobias feels very content. The air is crisp. The sun occasionally appears between the trees. The animals go about their business as usual. Or at least, that's what Tobias thinks. Of course, he lives in the city and doesn't really know what, for example, a squirrel's usual business is. He only knows pigeons, rats, and cockroaches. Their usual business is scurrying around for food and pooping everywhere. The animals here are hopping and flying around. The squirrel jumps from one tree to the next, seemingly soaring through the sky. If Tobias were paying closer attention, he would notice that all the animals are going in the opposite direction to him. But he isn't, so he just keeps going, knowing that he will eventually come to a town of some sorts.

He doesn't really know how much longer it will take, so he is pleasantly surprised when he sees a clearing just around a bend in the road. In the clearing stands a solitary house. It has a porch that goes right around it. As Tobias approaches the house, he notices a small shed attached to the right side. In front of the house is a drinking well with a bucket raised above it.

Tobias is a little thirsty, so he walks up the steps onto the porch and knocks on the door. He wants to ask whoever lives here if he can have some water. Unfortunately, nobody comes to open the door. He knocks again, but with the same result. Figuring that he isn't doing any harm, he goes back down the steps and crosses to the well. With the aid of a lever, he lowers the bucket into the water. As he is turning the lever to raise the bucket back up, a small figure appears behind him.

"What do you think you are doing?"

Startled by the sharp voice, Tobias lets go of the lever and the bucket drops down with a splash. Fortunately, the rope attached to the bucket doesn't drop. If it did, the person behind him would not be amused.

"I apologise," Tobias says as he starts to turn around. "I knocked but nobody answered the door..." Those last words fade away as he sees whom he is talking to. The tiniest person he has ever seen is standing in front of him. Involuntarily, his jaw drops and he just stares.

The tiny person crosses his arms. "What? You've never seen a leprechaun before?"

All Tobias can do is shake his head. He has walked through a portal into another land and has conjured up several things, which can only mean that magic is real. But somehow it never occurred to him that this might mean that mythical creatures actually exist as well.

"Have you looked your fill, lad?"

This seems to wake Tobias up. He quickly shakes his head. "I'm so sorry. I really didn't mean to be rude."

The leprechaun cocks his head. "You seem to apologise a lot. Is that a habit of yours?"

"Not really, no."

"Well," – the little man turns around and motions for Tobias to follow him – "you might as well come in. I have some water inside that's already been boiled and chilled." Suddenly, he stops and looks at Tobias. "You weren't planning on drinking straight from the well, were you?"

"Uhm, yes, I was."

"Completely daft." With great effort, the little man walks up the steps.

Just as Tobias starts to wonder why someone that small would live in a house like this, an explanation is given.

"Do you like it? I won it in a wager a few years ago. Would never have bought it myself, but never look a gift horse in the mouth is what my mum always said. I did make some minor adjustments, though."

It's only when they reach the top of the steps that Tobias notices the smaller door inside the normal-sized one.

"I'm Wally, by the way," the little man says, just before walking through the tiny door and closing it behind him.

Tobias is left standing outside, wondering what to do next, when he hears a few scratching noises from the inside. A little bit later, the big door opens, and he can just see Wally jumping down from a ladder.

"No offence, but Wally doesn't really sound like a leprechaun kind of name."

"None taken," Wally says as he leads the way to the living room. "My mother, rest her soul, had the mistaken idea that I would do great things, and so she gave me a great name." When he notices Tobias looking at him quizzically, he continues, "Well, a great name for our kind, anyway. I can assure you, there is no other leprechaun named Wally. She figured that if I was to do great things, I should have a name that stood out. She was right about that. I was bullied to no end in school."

They enter the living room. It is filled with human-sized furniture, but right in the middle of the room is an exact copy of the decor in miniature, as if made for a doll's house.

Wally watches Tobias taking in all the details and then looking at the rug in astonishment. He feels a word of explanation is necessary. "I liked the original furniture when I moved in, but it was just a tad too big, so I made copies. Do you like it?"

"It's amazing," Tobias says in awe.

"Thank you, lad." Wally walks to the rug and sits on the tiny sofa. "I did leave the original furniture where it was as well because the place would be very empty without it. Plus, it is immensely heavy. Wouldn't know how to get it out of the house, to start with."

Tobias is still standing in the doorway, not quite sure what to do.

"Still, it comes in handy when I have bigger company. Please, lad, sit down. You are putting a strain on my neck."

Happy to know what is expected of him, Tobias sits down on the big sofa.

"That's much better. Now, tell me. Who are you and why are you here?" Wally nestles down a bit on the sofa, preparing himself for his companion's entire life story.

"Well, my name is Tobias, and you could say I'm on holiday."

When Wally realises that no further explanation is coming, he is a bit disappointed. His mother always told him he was quite the chatterbox and that some people really weren't like that, but that didn't stop him from feeling disappointed whenever he met someone like that.

Tobias notices the change in Wally's mood but doesn't really know what else to tell him. Somehow, it doesn't seem like a good idea to tell his host that he stepped through a portal created by twirling a stick he found on the ground.

"Well," – Wally gets up from the sofa – "I do believe you were thirsty when I found you. I will get you that water I promised." He disappears through a small door in the big door that seems to lead to the kitchen.

Tobias stays on the sofa until his attention is drawn to a bookcase in the corner. He gets up and walks over to it, skimming the books' spines and titles. If he wasn't sure before, he is now: he is no longer in Kansas.

Suddenly, he hears Wally calling out to him. He goes through the door and finds his host on top of the kitchen counter.

"I just realised my glasses are too small for you. If you look in one of the cupboards, you'll probably find something more your own size."

Tobias does what he is told and quickly finds a glass. When he puts it down next to Wally, he notices the two miniature buckets of water on the floor. Pointing at them, he says, "Would you like me to, you know, pour?"

"Perfect." Wally steps down a ladder while Tobias goes down on his haunches and fills his glass. Wally holds up his own glass, and Tobias fills that one as well. Two Wally-sized buckets of water have nearly half-filled Tobias's glass. Hell, it's the thought that counts, isn't it? Unfortunately, Wally remembers just how much effort those two buckets took to fill. He is almost wishing he hadn't invited this stranger in. He is happy to have someone to talk to, but conversation-wise Tobias isn't living up to Wally's expectations, and now he is drinking all his water.

By the time they sit back down in the living room, each on his own sofa, Tobias's glass is empty. So, he suggests to his host that he can get some more water from the well for him. Wally smiles and happily agrees. Tobias walks back to the kitchen. Looking at the two buckets Wally uses, he figures that those won't do, so he looks around the kitchen and finds a human-sized bucket in one of the closets. He also finds a machine to filter the water without having to boil it on the stove. He takes that out and puts it on the floor in the middle of the kitchen. There is a small tap on the side of the machine, so he figures Wally will be able to use it too. Then he goes outside and starts to turn the lever to raise the well bucket, which is still in the water where he dropped it. He fills his own bucket and goes back inside, where he finds Wally staring at the machine in the middle of the kitchen.

"Do you have a candle?" Tobias asks.

Wally startles, but immediately pulls himself together. "I think there are a few in one of the drawers."

Tobias rummages through them. He finds two candles and a box of matches. Then he drops to his knees, places one of the candles in the appropriate place, and lights it. Opening the top of the machine, he pours the entire contents of his bucket into it. Wally's eyes widen at the thought of how long that much water will sustain him.

"It will probably take some time, but I think this will be faster than boiling the water and waiting for it to cool down again." Tobias is amused by the look on Wally's face.

"Right you are. Right you are."

"Let's go back into the living room." Tobias stands and opens the door.

Wally walks through it, still looking at the contraption in his kitchen. It is only when the door closes that he seems to snap out of it. They sit back down on the sofas.

"Thank you, lad. That's going to last me a very long time."

"It is the least I could do." Tobias settles down on the sofa and realises that his host is starting to grow on him.

Wally, in turn, decides that it isn't so bad to have this stranger around.

Five

Unicorns are Real Bastards

Petulia is having a lot of trouble keeping her purple broom steady. Miss Level, however, is a natural. She keeps going ahead and then turning back to her friend or waiting at the next bend in the road. Of course, with brooms they don't really need to stay on the road, but they figure that whoever is using – and spilling – magic is probably new here, and so more likely to stay on the path.

"Damn it. Stop flying back and forth. You are getting on my nerves." Petulia has both hands firmly on her broom. "If you must keep moving about, why don't you fly up ahead and see if you can find anyone?"

Miss Level smiles. "Of course, dear." And off she goes.

"Show-off." Petulia focuses all her attention on her broom. If she can just focus, she can keep it steady and she won't look like she still has her learning license. The shaking and abrupt stopping have made her feel a bit queasy as well.

But now that Miss Level is not around, Petulia is less distracted. Slowly, she begins to fly smooth and straight. Ah, finally. Then, just as she starts to feel confident, she looks up and sees Miss Level standing a bit down the road, waiting for her.

"Damn it." Abruptly, the broom shoots downwards, which causes the handle to stick in the ground and makes the broom flip over. Petulia lands flat on her back.

Miss Level drops her own broom and runs over to her friend. "Are you all right?"

"Perfectly fine. Just felt like resting for a bit." The fall has hurt Petulia's back quite badly, but she'll be damned before she shows any sign of pain.

Miss Level can see that the fall has hurt her friend, but she also knows how stubborn said friend can be. If Petulia says she's fine, then she's fine. Even though the grimace on her face clearly states otherwise.

"Just fine." Seeing the knowing expression on Miss Level's face and wanting to change the subject, Petulia asks, "Did you find anything?"

"All right, then." Miss Level stands up and walks back to the tree where she was standing before. When Petulia does not follow her, she shouts, "It looks like someone had breakfast here. There is some leftover bacon and eggshells." Feeling like quite the detective, she picks up the bacon. "It's cold, so I would say it was about an hour ago."

"How could you possibly know that?"

Illusion shattered, Miss Level replies, "All right, I don't know that. But I can still smell the magic that was used here, and we didn't see any new ripples so that must have been about an hour ago."

Petulia rolls her eyes. Of course, nobody can see it because she is still lying down.

Miss Level walks back to join her friend. Not really knowing what else to do, she lies down next to Petulia and waits patiently for her to be ready to stand and move on.

For her part, Petulia knows perfectly well that they don't have the time to lie around like this. She probes gently with her fingers to see if her back is all right. Quite sore, but nothing broken. Slowly, she sits up. "Right, then. Let's go."

Miss Level sits up as well and helps her friend to stand. "Do you want to walk for a bit?"

Relieved by that offer, Petulia just nods. She takes her broom in her right hand and starts to use it as a walking stick. This helps a lot and it doesn't require any special focus or talent.

As they pass the tree with the leftover breakfast beneath it, Miss Level quickly recovers her own broom and rejoins her friend, walking alongside her.

"You are right," Petulia remarks grudgingly. "It does smell like spilled magic here."

"Unmistakably."

"Any idea what we are going to do when we find the person responsible?"

"Not a clue." Miss Level regards her friend. "It was your idea to go after them. What did you have in mind?"

"No idea. I just know that we have to stop them before they wake up anyone or anything we really don't want walking around."

"Right." Miss Level isn't sure who or what Petulia is referring to, but she has been around long enough to know that some things really shouldn't be in this world.

"Correct me if I am wrong, lad, but you don't seem to be from around here." Wally figures that, if his companion isn't naturally inclined towards speaking, he might just need a push to open up.

"You are right. I'm definitely not from around here."

"The accent gave you away," Wally says. "That, and the fact that I am clearly the first leprechaun you have ever seen."

"Right again." Tobias decides he might as well share a few things with this character. "Where I come from, you don't really exist."

Wally is shocked. "What?"

"Well, you only exist in stories, myths, and generally only in Ireland." At Wally's confused look, Tobias continues, "Don't ask me why only in Ireland, because I honestly don't know."

After some thought, Wally says, "But you have heard of my kind before, yes?"

"Yes, I have."

"So, we must exist in your land as well. Otherwise, you would have no idea what I was, would you?"

"I guess."

"What is Ireland?"

"Well, it's a country in Europe." Tobias thinks for a while. "I don't really know that much about it. It has a lot of sheep. And it's generally acknowledged that Irish people drink a lot."

"Well, that explains it." Relief washes over Wally. "Only drunk people are completely honest. They would tell anyone that they saw a leprechaun." Noting Tobias's unbelieving look, Wally explains it further. "Sober people think too much about what other people think of them. They would rather believe they are mad than admit that they saw one of us. It is the same in the big cities here. That is why we always live in the forest. People in the city generally ignore us. Very hard to get a job. Impossible to keep one. Anything in sales is completely out of the question."

It sounds weird but it sort of makes sense, which makes Tobias wonder, "What about unicorns?"

"Oh, they are very real. Mean bastards as well. If you ever see one, make like a tree and leave."

Tobias leans in closer, eager for more information. "And faeries? Are faeries real?"

"Oh aye, gorgeous creatures. But stay away from pixies. They look a lot like faeries, I even think they are related somehow, but they are evil." A shudder goes through Wally just thinking about them.

"Ogres?"

"That is a tricky one. Long ago, ogres were banned. It was a whole lot of political nonsense which didn't really interest me so I don't know exactly what happened, but I heard that we created a new country for them and transported them to it. The local people didn't really like it but they were paid handsomely and we haven't heard from them since. So, I think the ogres are still around, but I can't say for sure. Best not to dwell on it, as my mum used to say, rest her soul."

"Huh. We had a similar situation where I come from. But instead of paying them we kind of let them fight it out among themselves. Literally."

"You don't say." Wally sips from his glass and waits for Tobias to continue. He's curious as to what else this giant man might think are mythical creatures.

Tobias suddenly thinks of his stick and the magic that comes with it. "Okay. Do you have witches?"

"Oh, sure. Too many of them, if you ask me. Some of them are really nice, like Miss Level. She's a sweetie. Doesn't live too far from here, if you want to meet her."

"Not really." Tobias wonders how much he can ask about witches before it becomes suspicious. There is one thing he really wants to know, though. "In the stories where I come from, witches always have wands."

"Is that so?" Wally replies. "And what, pray tell, are wands?"

"They are like small sticks they swish around to make magic, I guess."

Wally thinks about it for a while. "Of all the witches I know, I can't recall any of them having a small stick." Then he smiles and winks. "A few of the wizards do, though."

Innuendo – not something Tobias ever thought he would hear from a leprechaun. Then again, he never thought he would be talking to one either. It takes a while to clear his head. It also seems that his stick might not be from this world. Best not to talk about it, then. "All right. Now, these I am fairly sure don't exist: vampires."

"What are those?"

"They're sort of people that sleep during the day and wake up at night and feed on other people's blood."

"Oh, we just call them dracies. Harmless. Werewolves are a lot worse. They actually eat people. No one ever survives a werewolf attack. But a dracie attack is nothing. You might feel a bit faint afterwards, but that's it."

Tobias's head is about to explode. "I think I'm going to go check on the water." And with those words he gets up, picks up his and Wally's glasses, and trudges into the kitchen.

Petulia's improvised walking cane is starting to work against her. Her hand keeps slipping down it but she refuses to say anything.

Miss Level, who has noticed that her friend keeps slowing down, stops. "Wait a minute. I have an idea."

She takes the broom from Petulia and puts it next to her own. Mumbling a few Latin words, she lets her hands drift over the brooms. As her hands slide down them, the two branches entwine and form a thick two-seater broom with comfortable seats. A novelty, but very handy. Miss Level sits on the front seat and motions for Petulia to join her. Knowing that she won't be able to walk alone anyway, Petulia grudgingly sits sideways in the back seat, holding on to her friend. Miss Level pushes off and steers the broom at a leisurely pace further up the road.

"How did you think of this?" Petulia is astonished at the comfort of the two-seater, and by how smoothly it floats above the road.

"I don't know." Miss Level shrugs. "I just knew we needed another means of transportation and so I tried something new. Works pretty well, doesn't it?"

"Yes, it does." Feeling a little guilty for being so stubborn lately, Petulia mumbles, "Thank you", just loud enough for Miss Level to hear it.

In turn, Miss Level just smiles and says nothing.

The machine has finished filtering the water, so Tobias fills both glasses. Before he goes back to the living room, he looks around in the cupboard that holds the big glasses. If he remembers correctly, there was a sort of reusable bottle in there... Aha – found it. He quickly fills that as well and puts it on the draining board. When he leaves, he can take it with him.

As he enters the living room, Wally asks, "Do you have dragons?"

"Not that I know of."

"That is a pity. They are great for transportation."

Both men sit back and drink their water.

Deciding that there is no use in postponing the inevitable, Tobias says, "I think it's time for me to go."

A bit disappointed, Wally replies, "Oh, that's a shame. I was really enjoying your company, lad."

To his surprise, Tobias says, "Me too", and actually means it. The leprechaun is a funny little thing but he's also nice. Tobias is almost tempted to ask him to come along, but he's already starting to miss experimenting with his stick, so he leaves it at that. With a smile, he stands up. "Well, thank you for the water, and for correcting my misunderstandings about unicorns and such."

"You are welcome, lad." Wally smiles back. "If you ever pass by here again, do drop in."

"I will."

And with those words, Tobias leaves the room, grabs the bottle from the sink and steps out onto the porch. He takes a deep breath, revelling in the feeling of fresh air filling his lungs. Then he walks down the steps and continues his trip, walking around the bend and away from the house.

Six

On the Right Track

As Miss Level and Petulia float over the path, they suddenly notice that all of the animals are heading in the opposite direction. Now, usually they don't scare that easily, but seeing all the animals coming their way and passing them by without so much as a hello makes them feel uneasy.

Just to be sure, Petulia asks, "You're seeing them too, aren't you?"

"The animals? Yes, I am." Miss Level has the slightest inkling that they might not make it home before dinner, so she stops the broom and hops off.

The broom keeps floating, so Petulia, who is clearly wondering what her friend is doing, stays seated comfortably.

Miss Level walks up to a rabbit she befriended a while ago and asks what is going on.

"Can't you feel it?" the rabbit replies, glancing nervously behind him. "The evil one has woken up."

"The evil one? Are you sure?"

"There is no mistaking it." The rabbit tries to get past Miss Level, but she blocks his way.

"Can I ask a small favour of you?"

"I really don't have the time." He looks behind him again. "I want to be out of the forest before night falls."

"Oh, but it won't take much of your time. And you're already going the right way anyway."

"Well, what is it, then?" The rabbit is very anxious to leave.

"Could you just pop by our house and let Gabriel know I won't be home for dinner?"

The rabbit looks quizzically at her. "That is it?"

"Otherwise, he will be waiting for me, and I don't want him to starve." After a short hesitation, Miss Level adds, "And maybe tell him to keep the windows and doors shut."

"Sure. I can do that." Happy that this is just a small errand, the rabbit says goodbye and hops away.

Miss Level gets back on the two-seater broom. She pushes off again and they continue on their way.

Just around the bend, they can see the clearing where Wally lives. Petulia doesn't like the leprechaun very much. He always gets on her nerves because he can't stop talking and she can never understand anything he says. If they are going to stop at his place, she will be more than happy to let Miss Level do all of the talking. As Miss Level steers the broom in the direction of the house, Petulia rolls her eyes and hopes they won't stay too long.

Miss Level parks the broom near the porch. When she notices that Petulia isn't making any effort to dismount, she sighs and mumbles that she will be right back. She doesn't understand why

Petulia dislikes Wally. He is a nice enough person. One of the friendliest leprechauns Miss Level has ever met – they tend to be grumpy due to being ignored so much, and when they aren't ignored, they get suspicious. She walks up onto the porch and knocks on the door. There's a scurrying sound before the small door within the big door opens.

Wally pokes his head through the gap. "Why, Miss Level, to what do I owe the pleasure of your visit? If I had known I would get so many visitors today, I would have bought some crumpets."

"Oh, so you have a visitor right now?"

"No, unfortunately, you just missed him. Nice young lad. On holiday. I don't know where he is from but he knew very little of our land. Never saw a leprechaun before."

This could be just the person they are looking for, Miss Level thinks. Casually, she asks, "Did he say where he was going?"

"No, he didn't." Wally starts to get suspicious. He likes Miss Level a lot, even though she can be very weird sometimes. "Why do you want to know?"

"No particular reason."

Petulia has heard every word of their conversation and is anxious to leave, but realises that Wally won't let them go that easily. "We are part of the welcoming committee, Wally, and this young man has not received his basket of goodies yet. Now, where did he go?"

Wally doesn't believe them but wants to get rid of Petulia as quickly as possible. "He went back to the road and turned right." He turns to Miss Level. "He didn't do anything wrong, did he?"

She smiles at him. "No, Wally, you don't have to worry. He did nothing wrong."

Petulia mumbles, "Not that we know of."

As Miss Level passes her by, she elbows her friend to keep her quiet. Then she gets on the two-seater broom and pushes off. "Bye, Wally. See you on Tuesday for the bake sale."

Seven

Catching Up

At the same moment, Tobias clears the forest. The open road stretches out in front of him, flanked by green pastures filled with sheep. As he pays closer attention to the sheep, he notices that they are all trying to jump the fence to get away from the forest. He frowns. What has spooked them so much?

Looking around, he sees two women sitting on a floating broom. He soon makes the connection between the fleeing sheep and the floating women, and runs headlong across the grass.

"There he is!" he hears vaguely.

Crap! They're coming for him! Not really knowing where he's getting the strength from, he pumps his arms faster and races away.

"Go faster!" Petulia shouts. "He's getting away!"

Miss Level spurs the broom on. Slowly, they gain on the young man. When they've almost reached him, Petulia is so swept up in the moment that she stands up in her seat and jumps. She falls on top of the young man, causing both to tumble down. A small crack resounds.

The young man struggles to sit up, hindered in his movements by Petulia lying on top of him. "Get off me!" He pushes her aside, which causes her to roll a bit further away from him.

Before he can get to his feet, however, Miss Level hovers on her broom above him. "Don't be afraid. We mean you no harm."

"You just jumped me!"

"Of course we did. You were running away." Miss Level cocks her head. "Why did you run away?"

Tobias turns to look at the sheep. They are still trying to jump the fence, but don't appear to be trying to get away from these women. "I... The sheep... They were..."

Miss Level looks up and notices the sheep for the first time. "Oh, you thought they were running from *us*." She smiles. "No, silly. We could have told you that."

"So, what do you want from me?" Tobias is still sitting on the ground.

"Just a minute." Miss Level walks over to her friend. "Are you all right?"

"Fine, just fine," Petulia says, finding herself, for the second time today, lying flat on her back.

Miss Level regards her friend doubtfully. "I heard a crack before. Was it your back?"

"It might have been." Petulia gently probes her back with the fingers of her right hand. Nothing. Now, is it a good nothing or a bad nothing? She tries to sit up. No pain whatsoever. Perfect. She smiles at Miss Level and gracefully stands up. Then she walks over to Tobias. "We know you have been using magic, young man."

His eyes widen. "How did you know?"

"Because you are not practised in it."

He just frowns.

Petulia rolls her eyes. "Some of your magic is slipping away, causing ripples which can be seen or used by trained professionals."

"And that's bad?"

"Yes. That is bad."

He doesn't understand. "Why?"

"Because some people and some things really shouldn't have access to any kind of magic. Let alone the free kind."

"I didn't know." Tobias looks from one woman to the other and back again. "Honestly, I didn't."

Miss Level tries to smooth the waters, as it were. "We figured as much. That is why we came after you." She holds out her hand to help the young man up. "I am Miss Level and this is Petulia."

Her friend gives a half-hearted wave.

"We are witches. We could help you if you want."

"Why would you do that? Why not just tell me to stop?"

"General experience has taught us that people who come into contact with magic like it so much that they don't want to let it go."

A blush creeps up Tobias's cheeks.

"Nothing wrong with that, but then you really should train with a professional. They can teach you how to focus your magic and how to stop the spillage."

"And you want to teach me?" Tobias is a bit suspicious, but they don't seem all that harmful.

"If you'll let us."

He regards both women. The small one called Miss Level seems nice and genuine, but the tall one doesn't seem to like him that much.

As if reading his mind, Miss Level says, "Don't mind Petulia. She doesn't really like anyone. At least, not when she first meets them. But people tend to grow on her. And if they don't, she just ignores them."

"Like leprechauns?"

"Uhm, kind of, I guess," Miss Level replies hesitantly.

Tobias turns to Petulia. "I like leprechauns."

Immediately she replies, "How would you know? You have only just met one of them. And Wally isn't really representative of the entire species."

Tobias squints at her, then slowly turns to address Miss Level. "Can I choose which one of you teaches me?"

"Of course you can." Miss Level pats his arm.

"Then I want her to teach me." He points at Petulia.

Both women stare at him, mouths wide open. In unison, they ask, "Are you sure?"

He crosses his arms and nods. "Completely."

Miss Level turns to her friend. Without waiting for any response, she says, "Well, that is settled, then."

"All right," Petulia says. She has been suspicious of the young man since the moment she first laid eyes on him. "First lesson. Some witches or wizards need a focusing tool to help direct their magic. Do you have or use one?" She'll be damned, she thinks, if this little bugger is a natural who just happened to get in touch with his gift. Most wizards have an inkling when they are toddlers and then hone their talent throughout the rest of their lives.

Tobias hesitates for a moment. But if he really wants their help, he will have to tell them. "Yes, I do." He pulls the stick out of his back pocket and holds it up to the two women.

Immediately, they both step back and suck in a breath simultaneously.

Her eyes wide, Petulia asks, "Where did you get that?"

Clearly feeling uneasy under their scrutiny, Tobias hesitantly admits, "I found it."

"Where? Where did you find it?"

"On the street in Wakefield, Kansas."

The women look at each other.

"How could that be?" Miss Level asks. "That's not possible."

Their reaction causes Tobias to have a slight panic attack. He thrusts the stick at them, trying to get away from it. This only makes the witches jump back even further. Unfortunately, Petulia isn't quite fast enough: the stick touches her. A green spark appears and shoots up into the air, almost like a flare.

Miss Level and Petulia cry out, "No!", and watch the spark explode in the sky.

Tobias drops the stick as if it has suddenly grown too hot to touch.

His eyes open wide.

"It can't be." Power, such as he knew only in his heyday, rushes through him. He seems to vibrate with it. He smiles. "It has returned

for me." His smile grows even bigger. "And it has even found a witch for me."

He would rub his hands together and laugh maniacally if he weren't still stuck inside this tree.

"Soon. Very soon."

Eight

A Little History

Petulia, Miss Level and Tobias stare at the stick lying on the grass.

"Well, if there was any doubt, that definitely took it away." Petulia bends down and picks up the stick. Nothing happens. She gives it back to Tobias.

"Why isn't it sparking now?" Tobias doesn't know what to think of everything that just happened.

"It has done what it needed to do."

"Which is what exactly?"

"Sending a message to its owner that it is here and coming back to him."

Tobias is starting to get tired of the cryptic answers he is getting. "Look, if you don't explain everything to me right now, I am taking this stick and spilling more magic."

The women look at each other.

"It's only fair." Miss Level shrugs.

Petulia turns to Tobias. "Fine, but first things first: what is your name?"

"Oh, sorry." He holds out his hand. "I am Tobias."

The witches just stare at his hand; no idea what to do with it. Tobias rubs it on his shirt as if that was what he wanted to do all along.

Petulia rolls her eyes. "There's a tavern a bit further down the road. We will go there and eat something while we explain. Is that all right for you?"

"Sounds good." Tobias turns to walk ahead.

Miss Level watches her friend closely. "Will you be able to walk?"

Petulia smiles. "Yes. That last fall cracked my back, but in a good way."

Miss Level leans in and whispers, "How much are we going to tell him?"

"Everything, except the part we played." And with those words, Petulia follows Tobias before he can go the wrong way.

Miss Level sighs. She is fairly sure that they should tell this young man everything. She has a good feeling about him, and her feelings aren't usually wrong. She shrugs and starts after her companions.

The tavern is, let us say, quaint. A lot of dark woodwork, worn burgundy leather, not too many windows (the only light coming from candles spread throughout the space), and some shady characters at the counter. In spite of that, the place has a really good reputation. Milly, who owns it, is very friendly and her cooking is remarkable.

Petulia walks over to a small table in the corner from which they have an excellent view of the entire establishment. After Milly takes their order, Petulia settles down.

"Look, we don't have a lot of time, so here is the short version. About three hundred years ago, there was this great wizard named Melchior."

"Melchior?" Tobias asks.

Petulia squints at him. "If you are going to interrupt me, I am not telling the story."

He holds up his hands in surrender. "I apologise. Please, continue."

"Anyway, he was really powerful and quite handsome. Many women liked him. But he had his heart set on one particular witch. She, however, did not reciprocate his feelings. She thought he was stuffy and arrogant, and just generally didn't like him at all."

Miss Level coughs to help get her friend back on track.

"Right. So, she basically broke his heart. He didn't take it well. He started to demand higher fees for his services, which, of course, made people turn to other wizards. So he created diseases and ailments that no one else could cure. He also used a lot of myrrh in his potions, and everyone knows that that is just asking for trouble."

At that moment, Milly returns with their food and drinks: three house stews accompanied by three home-brewed ales. The divine smell of the stew fills their nostrils, so they quickly delve in, keeping the rest of the story for after they finish eating.

When they are fully sated, Petulia continues. "Myrrh is known for having a specific side effect: hallucinations. So, because of these new potions Melchior concocted, people were imagining terrible things. Wars broke out all over the land, families split up or even started killing each other. Let's just say, it was not pretty." She waits for a moment to collect her thoughts before continuing. She finishes her ale and motions to Milly for refills. "And then Melchior turned on his own kind. Even witches and wizards weren't safe any more."

Milly comes by and refills their drinks. The little pause is welcomed and they drink quietly from their tankards.

Then Petulia continues. "From that moment on, the Witches' Guild looked for a way to kill him. Unfortunately, it took a lot longer than expected and many witches and wizards were stripped of their powers and killed by him before the Guild could do anything. He had grown so strong and powerful that no spell in existence would work. So they looked for other ways, spells they could use to get him out of commission, so to speak."

Tobias, riveted by the story, forgets that he is not supposed to interrupt her. "What did they do?"

"They cast the most powerful sleeping curse ever created and locked him into a tree."

There is a slight pause.

"So," Tobias asks, "do you two belong to the Witches' Guild?"

"Yes, we do."

"So you helped put him in that tree?"

"Yes, we did."

He thinks for a little while. "Is that why the stick sparked?"

"Yes, it is."

"Okay. I have one more question. What does that stick have to do with it? Was it this guy's wand or something?"

"No. It's just part of the tree."

"The tree he is trapped in?"

"That would be the one." Petulia sips her ale, hoping that he is finished asking all these questions. Before they know it, he might actually ask the right one.

He crosses his arms. "Is Melchior a very common name here?"

"No," Petulia says. "There is only one. Why?"

"Well, I was just thinking..." Tobias hopes he doesn't make a complete fool of himself with what he is about to say. "Where I come from, we have a lot of folklore and myths. Now, Wally told me that a lot of the creatures from our stories actually exist here."

Miss Level is intrigued. "Go on."

"In one of our stories, there was a guy named Melchior. He was supposedly one of three wise men and they brought three gifts. One of them was myrrh." Tobias pauses for a few seconds. "Could it be the same guy?"

Petulia shrugs. "Sure. God used to do the same thing. I don't see why Melchior wouldn't. He had the means to, anyway."

Miss Level suddenly turns to her. "That's probably how the stick ended up in his world. If it was the last place Melchior went before we trapped him, he might have used the last morsel of his power to send a piece of the tree there, before he became completely dormant."

"And now he knows it's back." Petulia is not amused. "Damn it, he probably even harvested the magic that was spilt by our little genius and his stick here."

"Hey!" Tobias feels slightly offended. "I didn't mean to!"

Miss Level pats his arm softly. "Of course you didn't, dear."

"Of course he didn't," Petulia mocks. "But we still have to fix this."

With her other hand, Miss Level pats her friend's arm. "And we will." After a while of patting both Tobias's and Petulia's arms, she says, "We should go to the Guild."

Petulia's head snaps round to face her friend. "What?"

"We need to tell them what has happened. They probably already know part of it anyway."

"How?"

"You don't really think we were the only ones who saw the ripples, do you?"

"Good point." Petulia stares in the direction of the tavern door. "But why do we have to tell them?"

"We need their help to fix this."

Petulia sulks. She really doesn't want to go to the Guild. They still blame her for the last time. Suddenly, she realises something: she would bet everything that the Guild were the reason why her spells always went awry. They must have put some kind of hex on her. Jealousy, that is all it is.

Three hundred years ago, Miss Level and Petulia met in a rather abrupt way. Petulia was running through the forest and crashed into Miss Level, who was picking herbs. It was a strange meeting but somehow Petulia felt a little more at ease with Miss Level, albeit also a little more confused. She followed Miss Level to her home to have a cup of tea, and after about ten minutes they arrived at the gingerbread cottage where Miss Level lived.

Miss Level took a key out of her pocket and turned to Petulia. "I inherited it from an aunt. Apparently, she wasn't very kosher, but it is a nice place to live. Always smells amazing." She pushed open the door and walked in. "Although I do have to keep warning the children not to eat the walls." She pointed to the left. "You can already see a hole right there."

Petulia turned and, sure enough, there was a bite-sized hole right in the middle of the wall. She took in the entire room. They had entered what seemed to be a small living room. There was a big sofa taking up most of the space in the middle, with a coffee table in front of it. Behind the sofa was a door that led to who knows where. To the right, stairs led to the second floor. To the left, there was an open kitchen with a small dining table, four chairs, and a gigantic oven.

Miss Level was still standing next to her. "And I seem to always be hungry. I think it is from the smell." She smiled at Petulia. "Always high tea at my place." And then she shut her mouth. She had been talking non-stop since they'd started walking in the woods, but now she just stopped and gazed expectantly at Petulia.

Of course, Petulia had no idea what Miss Level was waiting for. So she just smiled back and said, "It's nice."

Miss Level sighed. Her smile wavered a little. "Why don't you tell me what you were running from in the woods and I'll see if I can help you? How does that sound?"

Petulia took a step back. She looked at Miss Level and cocked her head. She didn't know why but she had the distinct feeling that she could trust this woman, and that this woman could actually help her. But how to begin?

"I can tell by your expression that this is a story that requires something stronger than tea and biscuits." Miss Level turned on her heels, put her basket on the kitchen counter, and opened one of the top cupboards. Standing on the tips of her toes, she reached in and pulled out a bottle of red wine. "So we will have wine and something else." She opened another cupboard and took out two glasses. Putting the glasses and bottle on the table, she gestured to Petulia to sit. Then she turned her back to the table and rummaged through one of the kitchen drawers. "Where is it? Come on, where is the stinking thing?"

Petulia sat down hesitantly at the table, watching this weird short woman sliding stuff around in a drawer. She had come to the conclusion that this person must be a witch. How else would she have known that he wasn't following her?

"Aha!" Triumphantly, Miss Level raised a corkscrew in the air. "Found it." She turned and smiled before sitting down at the table. "Now, do you by any chance know how this contraption works?" She handed the corkscrew to Petulia.

Petulia took it and started to open the bottle. "How can you not know how this works? How have you been opening bottles?"

Miss Level looked away guiltily and mumbled something.

"What was that?" Petulia asked, just as she pulled the cork out of the bottle.

"I kind of…wish the cork away." Miss Level blushed.

"You what?" Petulia was sure she had misunderstood.

Miss Level rolled her eyes and sighed. "I used to wish the cork away, but I have recently found out that those corks don't just vanish. They reappear somewhere else."

The guilty look on Miss Level's face made Petulia smile. "So where did they end up?"

Her companion started to roll a strand of her hair between her thumb and forefinger. "The office of one of the wizards at the Academy."

"Which one?"

"God." Miss Level raised her eyes to look at Petulia, who immediately started to laugh. "What's so funny? He got fired because they all think he has a drinking problem."

Petulia continued laughing, putting her hands on her hips to ease the stitches she felt developing in her sides.

"It is not funny!" Miss Level argued, but the corners of her mouth were starting to tip up. "He had to move to Heaven to get away from his reputation."

Petulia put her head on the table as she shook with laughter. At this point, Miss Level was helpless to stop her, so she joined in. Ten minutes later, the last tear of laughter rolled down their cheeks and they looked at each other.

"Well," Petulia said, "you must not like him very much." She took a handkerchief from her pocket and dabbed her eyes.

"Apparently." Miss Level ran her sleeve over her cheeks. She stood up, opened the same cupboard in which she'd found the bottle, and took down a covered bowl. Lifting the cover, she put the bowl on the table. "This is something new I tried."

Petulia stared into the bowl. It was filled with small, slightly curled, yellow discs. "What is that?"

Miss Level reached into the bowl and popped one of the discs into her mouth. A crunching sound followed, and then she swallowed. "They are potato discs. I sliced the potatoes, put some oil and salt on them, and then put them in the oven." She gestured to the huge oven behind her. "What else are you supposed to do with something like that?" She shrugged and pushed the bowl towards Petulia.

Petulia grabbed a disc and popped it into her mouth. The salty taste filled her mouth as she started chewing. "Crunchy but good," she said as she finished the first of many discs.

Miss Level poured two glasses of wine and put one in front of her new friend. "So."

Petulia swallowed. "So."

"What happened?" Miss Level sipped from her glass.

Her companion first took a big gulp of wine, coughed a little, and then drew a deep breath. "Do you know Melchior?"

Miss Level nodded. Of course she knew Melchior. Who didn't? He was famous for his myrrh remedies. People came from far and wide to ask for his help. He was also an amazing wizard. And very handsome.

"Well," hesitantly, Petulia started to relay her story, "he was my mentor." She glanced at Miss Level to gauge her reaction, but she just smiled and nodded her encouragement. "I learned a lot from him. Really amazing things."

The more she told Miss Level, the calmer and more at ease she felt. She told her everything. She explained how she had met

Melchior at the Academy, and how he had taken an immediate interest in her. Of course, she had been ecstatic when he'd chosen her as his pupil. He had taken her with him on trips around the country to help sick people. She had been amazed by his talents, and had known that she would never live up to his standards. But then he had fallen in love with her, and she had fallen for his charm and his power. They had been together all the time. She had even moved into his house.

But after a year, she had started to notice something strange about his behaviour. He had no longer been content to help people. He had started to try some new things with the myrrh. She hadn't known what exactly, but she could feel that it was no longer what he was known for. She started to notice something odd about his customers as well. They would get this vague look in their eyes, as if they were unsure of what was real and what wasn't. During these experiments, Melchior would get this glint in his eyes. At first, Petulia had followed his lead, even though she hadn't been sure it was the right thing to do. She had learned some things that she shouldn't have learned, but she had convinced herself that it wasn't dark magic. It might have been 'dimmed light', but it wasn't dark. Unfortunately, the dark magic had an allure that Melchior could not resist. She could see it in his eyes. That glint...

She tried to draw him back to light magic, but realised she had waited too long. He was on the edge between light and dark and she didn't know what would make him choose one over the other. So, she decided to leave him. Maybe that would shake him out of it. But in the moment when she was about to tell him that she would leave if he didn't stop his experiments, he proposed to her. Her immediate reaction had been to recoil and stiffen. This was not what he had expected, and he grew angry. So angry. The glint took over his eyes, turning them blood red. He roared at her, yelling profanities and promises of all the pain she would endure for this. All she could do was turn and run away as fast as she possibly could.

Petulia stopped talking and looked down at her hands holding the stem of the wine glass.

"And that's when you ran into me," Miss Level finished.

"Yes."

Miss Level stared into her own glass, not quite knowing what else to say. She knew Melchior. She knew that he was a good man and a great wizard. She knew how many people he had helped. But she couldn't deny the feeling of unease she had felt right before meeting Petulia, although she sincerely hoped it wasn't justified. "I will help you," she said. "You are safe here."

Petulia's shoulders relaxed a little. She picked up her glass with shaking hands, and drank.

The following day, Petulia opened her eyes to find herself lying on a sofa. She turned her head and noticed two empty wine bottles on the coffee table. She couldn't recall when they had opened the second bottle; nor when they had moved to the sofa. Her head felt heavy and she was having trouble keeping her eyes open. She groaned. Wine shouldn't have this effect on her. She was a witch, damn it. Then she glanced at the coffee table and noticed the half-empty glass of whisky. Well, that would explain it.

"Morning, sunshine," Miss Level greeted her from the kitchen. She was mixing batter in a bowl and adding blueberries to the mix. "Want some pancakes? They will help with your hangover."

"I don't have a hangover," Petulia replied hoarsely. She cleared her throat and tried again. "I don't have a hangover." Better. Slowly, she stood and walked towards the kitchen table. How could Miss Level be this chipper; this active? What time was it?

"It is almost noon," Miss Level said, making Petulia wonder if she could read minds. "Now, sit down and I will get you a cup of tea and some pancakes." She put the bowl on the counter, turned to the exact same cupboard that had held the wine, and pulled down a box filled with all different kinds of tea, either loose leaf or prepurchased. She slid the box in front of Petulia before putting the kettle on the stove.

Petulia opened the box. How many different kinds of tea were there? She lifted every single one of the teabags until she found a plain black tea.

In the meantime, Miss Level had already made two pancakes and was pouring batter into her pan for a third one. She put a plate with the two pancakes in front of Petulia. "Here. Eat."

"Just tea will be fine," Petulia croaked.

Miss Level looked at her sternly. "Eat."

Really not feeling like it, but a little scared to argue with her, Petulia picked up a fork and started on the first pancake.

"So, I thought about everything you told me last night." Miss Level slid another pancake from her pan onto Petulia's plate. "Do you know what Melchior was going to do today?"

Petulia frowned. "No. Why?"

"Well, I thought we could maybe go to his place and check out what he has been doing since you left." Miss Level glanced at her new friend. "If we need to warn people about him, we should know what to warn them about."

Petulia looked at her. "I don't know. I am not very keen on going back there. You should have heard the things he shouted."

"I understand. But he didn't come after you, did he?"

"It would appear not."

Miss Level shrugged. "So maybe it was all talk and he isn't going to do anything."

"Or maybe he is planning something big." Without realising it, Petulia finished the last of the first two pancakes, making her feel remarkably better than before. "These were really good."

"Don't sound so surprised. My aunt, who used to live here, was a baker. It's in my blood." Miss Level flipped a fourth pancake onto Petulia's plate before turning off the stove and sitting down to eat something herself. "If he is planning something big, we should try to find out what."

That idea seemed to make sense to Petulia, so she nodded her reluctant consent.

"Great – I will get all our supplies ready. Right after I finish eating." Miss Level stood up again and lifted the kettle from the stove, just as it started to whistle. "Tea?"

Petulia lifted her cup in response.

Nine

The Man Cave

An hour later, the two women put on their coats and left the cottage, pulling the door tightly shut behind them. Then immediately Miss Level stopped, causing Petulia to bump into her yet again.

"Damn it. Why are you just standing here?" Petulia frowned at her new friend.

"Because I don't know which way to go," Miss Level explained. "You have to lead the way."

Petulia huffed and stomped past her companion. To be completely honest, she was still unsure that this was a good idea. It had sounded good when they were inside the cottage, but so had that glass of whisky last night. Well, she couldn't back out any more, and some part of her really did want to know what Melchior was up to.

"Hey, wait for me!" Miss Level's voice floated towards her.

Petulia glanced back and saw Miss Level practically running to catch up with her. Right, her legs were shorter. Must remember that. She waited until the other woman was at her side. "Sorry," she mumbled.

But Miss Level just smiled at her. "Don't worry, I'm actually quite used to it."

They continued walking: Petulia really trying to slow down her pace; Miss Level really trying to pick up hers.

"So, where does he actually live?" Miss Level didn't really like silences, especially when two people were clearly together. She had heard of comfortable silences – you know, when you are so comfortable with each other that you don't need words – but she had never had one of those. That could be because she just really liked talking. In a way, she was happy that she had met Petulia. Now she had someone to talk to. Until she went away, of course. Well, they would just cross that bridge when they reached it.

"There is a big cave in the mountain. So big that Melchior has built a castle in it." Petulia thought for a moment. "That should probably have been a warning bell." She shook her head. "Completely missed it."

"Right." For a moment, Miss Level didn't know what to say. That did not happen very often. "Uhm, so is there a secret passage or will he spot us right from the start? If he is at home, of course."

"If he is home, he will spot us. He doesn't have a back door or anything like that." Unconsciously, Petulia picked up her pace again, eager to get this over with.

Miss Level hurried to stay with her, but she didn't mention it to her companion. She could see the anxious look on Petulia's face. Maybe she should try to lighten the mood. It couldn't be easy to go back to your ex and spy on him. "What did you think of the pancakes?"

"What?" Petulia gave her a confused look. "What are you talking about?"

"Did you like them?" Miss Level asked. "It was the first time I made blueberry pancakes so I am curious about your feedback."

"They were fine." Petulia started to wonder if the woman next to her was all right in the head. She glanced at her. It would explain why she wanted to go to Melchior's place after everything Petulia told her last night.

"Good. Good." Miss Level tried to find another subject to talk about. "So, what do you think of God?"

"Why are you asking about God?" Even more confused, Petulia just kept walking.

"Well," Miss Level said, "when I talked about him last night, you seemed to know him."

"Oh." A small smile appeared on Petulia's face. "No, I don't know him. But I have heard of him and his reputation for drinking. It was just funny to hear that it wasn't really true."

"Oh."

Well, that was a conversation stopper. To the annoyance of Miss Level, they walked further in complete silence. There must be something that Petulia liked to talk about. Perhaps Miss Level shouldn't push so hard and fast for conversation. Determined that she would find a topic Petulia liked (but just not right now), Miss Level gazed around the forest. Bees were buzzing, birds were flying, squirrels were jumping from tree to tree. One more day and summer would begin. Just to be sure, she raised her pinkie again. She nodded – yes, one more day. Petulia didn't notice any of this. Her mind was fully occupied with Melchior. She really hoped he wasn't at home, because if he was, she might just turn around and run away screaming.

After about an hour's walk, they arrived at the entrance to the cave. Petulia gazed inside anxiously, not getting too close. She didn't really see anything. She crept a little closer to the side wall and peered around the corner. Nothing; no movement whatsoever. Miss Level, who had, surprisingly, been silent during all of this, watched her companion and followed in her footsteps. Together, the women moved silently into the cave, sliding along the wall, which was quite difficult as it was formed entirely from jagged rock.

Miss Level's coat snagged on a pointy rock. "Umph!" With her next step, she jerked back.

"Ssshhhh." Petulia turned to her and, seeing Miss Level struggle with her coat, took a step back and helped her untangle herself.

"Thank you," Miss Level whispered.

"Ssshhhh," Petulia repeated. Then she turned again and continued further into the cave.

After ten minutes, they reached a large chamber in the cave. A huge castle stood in the middle of it. Everything was dark.

Miss Level's head popped out from behind Petulia. "I don't think anyone is home," she whispered.

Petulia stared at the castle a little while longer. "I think you are right." She took a deep breath and stepped forward. "Follow me."

The two women walked slowly up to the main entrance: a massive wooden door. They stopped before the closed door.

"Now what?" Petulia turned to Miss Level.

"You don't happen to have a key, do you?" Miss Level asked.

"Are you serious?" Petulia put her hands on her hips, still whispering. "We came all the way out here and you don't even know how to get into the place?"

"Of course I do," Miss Level huffed. "It would just be a little easier if you had a key, so I thought I'd ask." She put the bag she'd brought with her on the ground, bent down and rummaged in it, then pulled out an ancient-looking key and a candle. As soon as the candle was lifted out of the bag, it caught light. Miss Level stood up. She held the key above the candle flame, closed her eyes and waited.

Just as Petulia was about to ask what was going on, Miss Level blew out the candle. The smoke circled the key and then floated towards the keyhole in the door. The key in Miss Level's hand transformed a few times until it was just the right shape and size. The smoke disappeared and Miss Level opened her eyes. She looked at the key and smiled.

"Well, that wasn't too hard." She handed the key to Petulia, who accepted it hesitantly before sliding it into the keyhole and turning it. A soft click resounded.

"Huh," was all that managed to come out of Petulia's mouth. She gently pushed open the door while Miss Level put her things away and lifted her bag.

*

The interior of the castle was dark, but the moment Petulia slid a foot over the threshold, several torches, hanging from the walls, lit up.

"That is very handy," Miss Level remarked. She looked around and took in the decor. The walls were made of granite bricks – big ones. The doors were dark wood. Several tapestries hung on the walls. Miss Level stepped closer to look at one of them.

"He has replaced them," Petulia stated. "That was quick."

"So, they weren't always these gruesome death scenes?" Miss Level shivered before turning away.

"No, they used to be forest scenes. You know: lots of sunshine coming through the canopy, and animals eating or playing on the ground." Petulia shrugged. "I didn't really like them, but these are a lot worse."

Another shiver ran through Miss Level. "Let's just keep going." She turned to the first door. "This way?"

"Not unless you want the kitchen." Petulia moved past her, towards the end of the entrance hall. A narrow staircase led them down into the cellars. "His workspace should be around the corner in that direction," she said as she reached the bottom step and pointed into the dark corridor.

"That won't do." Miss Level opened her bag and pulled out the candle again. As before, it immediately caught light. "That's better."

Petulia shook her head in astonishment. She'd known that this woman was a witch the minute she had met her, but this was some weird magic. Nothing Melchior or the Academy had ever shown her.

"What?" Miss Level frowned.

Petulia just shook her head again. "Nothing." She took the candle from Miss Level's hand and walked into the corridor, lighting the way.

When they rounded the corner Petulia had mentioned before, they stepped into a completely empty room.

"What the…" Petulia walked to the centre of the room and turned around. Several circles later, she stopped and stared at her companion. "I don't understand. Yesterday, this place was filled with books." She pointed to the walls. "And a big, heavy wooden table." She waved her hand to the middle of the room. "And magic ingredients." She pointed to another wall. "And…and… and…now it's all gone."

"I am not so sure about that." Miss Level squinted her eyes and slowly moved her gaze from one side of the room all the way to the other.

Petulia just stared at her. "What are you doing?"

Surprised, Miss Level immediately looked at Petulia; normal gaze, no squinting. "What do you mean, what am I doing? I'm checking for magic." She squinted again and continued to look around the room.

Curious to see what Miss Level could possibly be sensing, Petulia also squinted and looked around. "I don't see anything."

"You don't?" Miss Level crossed the room to where Petulia was standing and squinted again. "How can you not see anything? There is the table you mentioned, and the books on the walls, and the ingredients at the other end and… Did you mention a cupboard?"

"No."

Miss Level turned to Petulia, still squinting. "Oh, now I see."

"What? What do you see?" Anxiously, Petulia grabbed her friend's sleeve. "Tell me what you see."

Miss Level startled at the intensity of Petulia's pleas. "He has blocked everything. He put a spell on his workspace so that only he can see what he is working on. But he has put an extra block on you."

Petulia just stared at her, her mind reeling, several thoughts coursing through her head. "You said a cupboard?"

"Yes."

"There was never a cupboard in this room."

"Ah." Miss Level hesitated just a little before continuing. "Apparently, that is what he didn't want you to see." She turned her head to the far wall and squinted again. "By the looks of it, it has been here for quite a while. There are several cobwebs hanging from the sides."

"Can you see what is in it?"

"No, I am afraid I can't." Miss Level shrugged apologetically. "I can see the cupboard but unless I do some major magic here, I can't open it." Before Petulia could suggest that she start doing major magic, Miss Level continued, "And I am pretty sure he has blocked the use of magic here as well. Well, except for his own, of course."

"So we came all the way out here for nothing."

"Not for nothing. We learned one very important thing." Miss Level put her arm around her new friend, who stiffened slightly at the contact. "We learned that he was already heading to darkness. You didn't have anything to do with it."

Petulia sighed. "So now what?"

Miss Level lifted her bag higher on her shoulder and headed towards the door. "Now we get out of here and find some other witches and wizards so that we can tell them the good news about Melchior."

"Good news?" Petulia followed her down the corridor.

Miss Level shrugged again. "I was being sarcastic. Thought I might try it. Doesn't really work for me."

After leaving the castle and cave without any hindrance, Petulia and Miss Level made their way back through the forest to the gingerbread cottage. Miss Level did not attempt any more small talk, sensing that Petulia would not appreciate it.

Petulia was deep in thought. She was surprised that they had been able to walk into the castle without much trouble. After the goodbye Melchior had given her the day before, she had expected him to be plotting something. But to leave his home unprotected? That was weird. He had always been very protective of his things. She remembered how one time she had picked up his pen to write a stupid note. Wow, the anger in his voice had been palpable. But now...nothing? He must be up to something. Maybe he had got another place that she didn't know about? It was possible. There had been times when he had disappeared for a couple of days and wouldn't tell her where he had been. Maybe he had a secret lair. But how to find it?

"Do you think we could scry for Melchior?" Petulia looked expectantly at Miss Level.

Miss Level jumped, not expecting any sound from the woman walking next to her. "What?"

Petulia did not notice. "I was thinking about how easy it was for us to enter his cave and his castle."

"So?"

"What if he has another place where he practises his magic? More specifically, his dark magic?" Petulia scratched her head. "There were times when he would go away for days and I would not know where he had been." She shrugged. "I just thought he might have a hideout of some sort."

Miss Level cocked her head. "I suppose he might."

"So, could we scry for him?"

"I'm not sure." Miss Level took a deep breath. "He is a very powerful wizard. I think he might be able to sense someone looking for him. Or he might even block any scrying magic, like he blocked his workspace."

Petulia's shoulders slumped. "Right. Of course."

Always the cheery person, Miss Level smiled. "But that doesn't mean we can't try."

"You don't think it is a bad idea?"

"Oh, I absolutely do." Miss Level nodded vigorously. "That's why we won't be the ones doing the scrying." She winked at Petulia and started to walk faster.

"What do you mean?" Petulia raced to keep up with the short woman. "Who is going to do it?"

The only reply she got was a big smile.

Ten

Getting Some Help

When they entered the cottage, Miss Level immediately put her bag on the kitchen table and started rummaging through one of the drawers in the kitchen.

"Damn it." Petulia put her hands on her hips as she watched Miss Level going around the kitchen. "Will you tell me what you are doing?"

Finally, Miss Level pulled out a piece of parchment and a quill pen. She put them on the kitchen table before going through the door behind the sofa in the living room. Petulia, who was getting very curious and didn't want to miss a thing, followed her.

They were standing in a small library with hundreds of books on shelves across from the door. There was a small desk with one chair against the right-hand wall. The rest of the room was empty. Miss Level went to the desk, picked up a bottle of ink and left the room. Petulia forgot her annoyance at being left out momentarily. She stepped closer to the bookshelves. There were books on alchemy, geology and history, as well as magazines and encyclopaedias of magic. She stood in awe in front of the books.

Melchior had had an amazing selection of books, but they were all about magic. Some of them were also on these shelves, but Miss Level's collection was a lot more varied.

Miss Level popped her head around the door. "I thought you were coming."

Petulia just waved her hand at her, muttering, "Yes, yes. Coming."

Another smile took over Miss Level's mouth. "So, you like my collection?"

"Yes, it's amazing." Petulia turned to her. "Have you read all of them?"

"Not yet. Those, I still have to look into." Miss Level pointed to the top shelf. "But I can't reach them." She turned back towards the door. "That reminds me to get a ladder. I will add it to my grocery list." And with those words, she exited the room.

Petulia shook her head. "Such knowledge. I wonder if she even remembers everything from those books." The right-hand corner of her mouth lifted in a smirk. "I could have some fun with this. Quizzing her about everything." Suddenly, she heard the scratching of a pen on parchment, and rushed out into the living room.

Miss Level looked up as she finished her note. "So you *do* want to know what is happening." She smiled as she folded the parchment in half, turned it in her hands, folded it in half again, and put it neatly on the table.

Petulia came closer. "What did you write?" She reached out her hand to pick up the parchment, but Miss Level slapped it away.

"Don't touch," she said sternly, before lifting her bag off the table and bringing the candle out yet again. She put the bag on the floor as she carefully held up the lighted candle. Her hand slid over to the folded piece of parchment. She picked it up, closed her eyes, and mumbled a few foreign-sounding words.

Petulia tried to understand what she was saying but only picked up the odd word here and there. *Accercio. Voco.* Heaven and God. Her eyes widened. Miss Level was calling on God? Why would she do that? Before Petulia could say anything, Miss Level held the folded piece of parchment to the flame of the candle. It immediately caught fire and burned to ash. Petulia watched the black ashes float towards the kitchen table.

"Can you explain to me why you would call on someone who probably hates you?"

Miss Level frowned and cocked her head at her companion. "Why would he hate me?"

"Oh, please," Petulia replied incredulously. "You were the reason he lost his job and had to move to a different city."

Miss Level shrugged. "He doesn't know that."

"What?" Petulia stared at her. "How could he not know that?"

"I don't think anybody knows. Well, except you." Miss Level's eyes widened. "You won't tell him, will you?"

"Of course I won't." Petulia waited for just a second before continuing, "Just like you won't tell him that I rejected Melchior when he proposed to me, and that is what sent him over the edge." Her gaze bored into Miss Level's eyes, and Miss Level swallowed heavily.

"Why not?" Miss Level asked quietly.

"Because that is none of his business." Petulia kept watching her new friend, but a nervous edge formed on her words. "As a matter of fact, it is nobody's business. The only reason I told *you* is because we met right after it happened." She noticed Miss Level's shoulders slump. Crap – she must have said something to hurt her feelings. Honestly, she was never any good at recognising feelings.

"Oh." Miss Level turned around to pick up the dishcloth. "Of course. I understand. Mum's the word." She ran the tap and held the cloth under the streaming water, taking a moment to get herself together. Silly cow. It was not like they were friends. They had just met, for Pete's sake. Although what Pete had to do with this, she had no idea. She took a deep breath, turned back to Petulia and smiled at her. "I won't say anything to anyone."

Petulia watched Miss Level wipe down the kitchen table, expertly removing the soot from the burned parchment, before returning to the sink and rinsing out the dishcloth. So, she *hadn't* said anything wrong?

Petulia was still frowning when someone knocked on the door.

"That was fast." Miss Level threw down the dishcloth and went to answer the door.

Opening it, she found an extremely pissed-off God standing on her doorstep. "You *vocoed* me?" He barged in. "How dare you?"

"Hello to you too, God." Miss Level gently closed the door. She was familiar with God's outbursts. This was nothing to worry about. If he'd known that she was behind the corks ending up in his office, he wouldn't have even entered the cottage. He would have found a way to avoid coming, even if it had meant tying himself to a tree until the spell had passed.

"You know how I hate being *vocoed*." He stomped over to the sofa and sat down with a huff.

Miss Level smiled at him. "I wouldn't have done it if it wasn't an emergency."

"An emergency? Really?" God was a lot better at sarcasm than Miss Level. "Just like it was an emergency when you found that spider in your bath? Or when you needed someone to taste your potato discs, or whatever you call them?" He crossed his arms in front of him.

"Well, I know how much you like to be a saviour for damsels in distress, and how much you like to eat." Miss Level shrugged. "I didn't think you would mind."

It was at that moment that God turned his head towards the kitchen and noticed that someone else was in the room. He blinked and dropped his arms. "Petulia?"

"How do you know my name?" Petulia asked, but no reply came forth.

Miss Level stepped a little closer to the sofa. "God?" Another step closer, as if she were reluctant to frighten him. "How do you know Petulia?"

Slowly, God turned back to Miss Level. "Only by name." He looked at her and squinted. "How do *you* know her?"

"Don't you dare squint your eyes at me." Miss Level wagged her finger at him, causing him to stop it immediately. "We met yesterday." She glanced at the other woman. "She is the reason I called you."

"*Vocoed.* Not called." God's temper rose again slightly. "Calling would have been the nice way to do this, but no! Not Miss Level. She doesn't call. She *vocos*!" He yelled the last words at her.

A light purple glow started to radiate from Miss Level as she glared at the tiny man on her sofa.

God promptly swallowed his next words and held up his hands in surrender. "Just kidding."

Petulia's mouth dropped open as she stared at her new friend. Wow! How did she do that?

But the moment God said those last words, Miss Level smiled and the purple glow disappeared. "Oh. All right, then." She sat down on the sofa next to him, not noticing him sliding a little further away from her. "Petulia, why don't you pull up a chair from the kitchen table and join us?" Miss Level looked at her, all normal like.

Petulia shook herself. She must have imagined the glowing. She turned and grabbed a chair.

Miss Level turned to God as Petulia put the kitchen chair next to the sofa and sat down. "So," she sighed, "we have something to tell you that you might not want to believe."

God glanced uneasily between the two women before nodding to encourage them to tell their story.

As Miss Level finished the tale – leaving out the proposal, of course – she noticed that God and Petulia had fallen silent. "Did I tell it all right?" She looked at Petulia.

"Yes, that is just the way it happened." Petulia nodded and glanced at God.

God folded his arms across his chest again. "So, you are telling me that a man I have known since I was a little boy has just upped and decided to go dark?"

"Well, no, not really," Petulia said. "It sort of happened gradually, but by the time I figured it out, it was too late." She looked down at her hands folded in her lap.

God stood up and started pacing. "You are right, Miss Level. I don't believe you. Why would I?" He gestured wildly with his arms. "You are talking about a man that I consider a close friend. Someone I have a history with. A good history. I know this man. He is good. I have seen him help people. I have *helped* him help people."

Petulia frowned at him. "How long ago was this?"

"What?" God stopped pacing.

"How long ago was this? Because I lived with him for the last couple of years and I never saw you before you walked through that door." She pointed to the front door for emphasis.

God sputtered. "Well, that…that…does not matter. It doesn't mean anything. I still know the man. And I still think you are wrong."

Petulia rose from her chair, strengthened in her resolve. "Damn it, we just said it happened gradually over the last few years. If you haven't seen him in that time, then you can't know, now, can you?" She glared at the little man in front of her. "People change."

Petulantly, God sat back down on the sofa. "Well, I still don't believe you."

Miss Level, who had been waiting for the right moment, said quietly, "I understand that you don't believe us. It is a crazy story anyway."

Petulia glared at her. "What?"

Looking up at her, Miss Level continued, "You have to admit that it does sound a little far-fetched."

Petulia's only response to this was the dropping of her jaw.

"Look," – Miss Level slid closer to God and put her hand on his arm – "why don't you…oh, I don't know…scry for him or something…and put our minds at ease?" She glanced at Petulia, and was happy to see realisation hit her. "Then we can just put this thing behind us and move on, and we will never speak of it again. Especially not to Melchior, the good man – he will be so offended." She shook her head lightly.

"That's a great idea." God nodded smilingly at Miss Level, before turning to Petulia with a scowl. "We will immediately prove this story to be false."

Petulia gritted her teeth. Granted, it was beautiful the way Miss Level had just played this man, but did she have to make Petulia out to be the bad guy here? Still, it didn't matter. She would just have to bite her tongue until after God had scried.

Innocently, Miss Level asked, "Do you have your own scrying materials with you?"

"Of course I do." God rummaged in his pockets. "I never leave the house without my field kit."

He took out a soft piece of cloth and a piece of quartz on a string. He put the cloth on the coffee table, flattening it out so that it covered about half of the table. Then he scooted a little closer and held his left hand above the cloth. Closing his eyes, he raised his hand until it was about fifty centimetres above the cloth. Then he opened his eyes, took the quartz with the string attached in his other hand, and held it above his still-outstretched hand. Slowly, he released the string, letting the quartz drop smoothly towards his left hand. The fingers of that hand opened and the rock passed right between his middle finger and his ring finger until it hung about ten centimetres above the cloth. With his right hand, he started to move from side to side, creating a pendulum with the quartz that moved over the entire piece of cloth on the table. He closed his eyes again while he continued this movement.

After about five minutes, Petulia frowned. She wasn't a good scryer herself, but shouldn't he have found Melchior by now? She glanced up at Miss Level to gauge her reaction. The other woman was gazing intently at the quartz crystal.

Another five minutes passed. God started to frown as well. He took a deep breath and slowly blew it out. Then he stopped moving his right hand, letting the quartz swing until it finally came to a halt.

Miss Level followed the quartz until its last twitch. "You couldn't find him, could you?"

Reluctantly, God opened his eyes. "No, I couldn't." He hesitated. "It's as if he has vanished from the world." He stared at his scrying materials in confusion. Was the pendulum broken? Had he done something wrong?

"So what does that mean?" Petulia asked.

"Well, it means that Melchior is not in this world," Miss Level stated plainly.

Petulia put her hands on her hips. "Well, is he coming back?"

"I don't know." Miss Level cocked her head to one side. "I should think so, but who knows when that will be?"

Finally, when he was absolutely certain that he hadn't done anything wrong, God lowered his hands and started to put his things away. "I don't understand. Where could he be?"

"He's not dead, is he?" Petulia wondered aloud.

God snorted. "Of course not. And even if he were, we would still be able to find him." He rolled his eyes. And she called herself a witch? Everybody knew that. It was basic knowledge. What did Melchior see in her?

Miss Level watched him. "Would a good person vanish like that? Would he hide…wherever he is?"

God's cheeks started to turn red. It was not with embarrassment, nor with anger. It was with shame. He had defended the man, but of course a good person wouldn't hide like this. Miss Level knew that. He grumbled a confirmation that no one understood, but they got the gist of it.

"So, do you believe us now?" Miss Level put her hand on his arm again.

"I don't *not* believe you," God conceded. "But to *actually* believe you, I will need more proof."

At that point, Petulia lost her patience with him. "As we can't find him, we can't find out what he is planning. And if we don't know what he is planning, we can't plan anything of our own to stop him."

A little confusing, but Miss Level understood what her new friend was saying. "So, we wait him out?"

Petulia shrugged. "I don't think there is anything else we can do right now. Do you?"

Miss Level thought about it for a while. "Not really, no." She turned to God. "If you hear of him, or if you hear about some strange stuff going on that might be him, will you let us know?"

He grumblingly agreed.

"Good." Miss Level nodded. "And we will let you know if we hear anything." She stood up. "Well, thank you for coming." And with those words, she let the somewhat confused God out of her house.

On her return, Petulia shook her head incredulously. "Wow, you really have that man wrapped around your finger, don't you?"

Miss Level smiled. "As long as he doesn't notice it himself, I don't see the harm in it."

Petulia sighed. "So what do we do now?"

Miss Level shrugged. "I guess we wait." She walked into the kitchen and started taking down pots and pans.

"Right." Petulia looked around, thinking that she had probably already overstayed her welcome, but reluctant to leave.

"How about you start peeling those potatoes?" Miss Level pointed to a heaped pile of the things in a corner. "We will have dinner, and then I will make up the guest bedroom for you."

Petulia froze. "What?"

"It seems to me that we should stick together until we find out what Melchior is planning."

"Right." Petulia turned to the potatoes with a little smile on her lips, and bent down to pick a few of them up.

Eleven

An Unusual First Day of Summer

Summer had come in with full force. The sun beat down with a glaring heat. The birds that had been flying around, carefree, the day before were now hiding out under the canopy, trying to find any slice of shade.

Miss Level opened her bedroom window, only to quickly close it again. "Wow, that won't help at all." She pulled the curtains closed. "But I was right." She smiled and turned towards the door to go downstairs.

Petulia was already in the kitchen, making breakfast. Or trying to, anyway. The kitchen was a complete mess. The table and counter, as well as Petulia, were coated with some sort of powder; presumably flour. "Damn it," Petulia muttered. "Why won't this stupid thing work?" She pushed a button on the stove repeatedly, trying to get a fire ignited, but nothing happened. "Damn it. These new contraptions are stupid. What is wrong with a regular fire?"

Suddenly, she realised that she was no longer alone in the kitchen. Hastily, she turned around to find Miss Level sniggering at her. Miss Level stepped up to Petulia, grabbed a matchbox from the drawer next to the stove, and lit a match before holding it to the stove pit and pressing the button again. Immediately, the stove pit caught the flame.

Miss Level turned to Petulia, still sniggering just a little. "I appreciate the effort." She held out her hand for the pan Petulia was holding. "But I can see you're not really a great cook, are you?"

Petulia relinquished the pan into Miss Level's capable hands before sinking down onto one of the kitchen chairs. "Not really, no." She looked at the table and the counter. "I made a real mess, didn't I?"

"Yes, you did." Her friend stared into the bowl, which contained batter for blueberry pancakes. She dipped her finger in it and tasted it. Not too bad.

Petulia sighed. "I will clean all this up. Should I get rid of the batter as well?"

"No, it's fine," Miss Level replied. "I can work with this." She smiled and set to it, while Petulia cleared the table as promised.

The pancakes turned out quite well, although they were a bit too salty. The two women ate and discussed their plan for the day.

"I was going to go to Edmundtown to get some supplies. Do you want to come with me?"

"Sure," Petulia mumbled with a full mouth, surprised at how well the pancakes had turned out.

Miss Level smiled at her. "You should probably clean up before we leave."

Only then did Petulia glance down and notice all the flour that covered her. Her eyes widened. "Cripes."

"How have you survived for so long?"

"There were always other people preparing the food when I was young. And when I went to the Academy, they had their own cooks as well. And Melchior, well, he just magicked it up."

Miss Level frowned. "He magicked up *food*?" She shook her head. "What a waste of energy."

Petulia shrugged. "I was just happy I didn't have to cook it myself, so I didn't think anything of it."

"All right, that settles it." With a decided air, Miss Level put down her fork on the table. "I am teaching you how to cook."

Again, Petulia's eyes widened but she didn't say anything.

"We will start with some basics, like soups and salads, and breakfast stuff, like pancakes and waffles." Miss Level nodded. She liked this plan. "And it will give us something to do until… you know." Her voice trailed away.

"Yeah, I know." Petulia gazed at the rest of her pancake, suddenly feeling a lot less hungry.

After breakfast, the women took their bags and left the house through the front door. The sun beat down on them, but they started walking anyway. It wasn't long before they rolled up their sleeves and hiked up their skirts to let the occasional breeze flow through.

They were about halfway through the forest when a sudden chill swept over them.

Miss Level stopped in her tracks. "That doesn't seem right." She glanced around, squinting her eyes in case she could pick up anything weird. Nothing.

A cold breeze made Petulia shiver. "What is going on?"

Both women dropped their skirts and rolled down their sleeves. The sun was still out, but it didn't seem to be giving out any warmth any more. The air chilled, and a few clouds started to roll in. Unconsciously, Petulia and Miss Level stepped closer to each other for warmth.

Miss Level noticed their breath forming small clouds. "How is this happening?" She turned to look up at Petulia. "It is the first day of..." She fell silent as she watched a single snowflake float down and land on Petulia's hair.

Petulia hadn't noticed anything. "The first day of what?"

"Summer." Miss Level was stunned. Snow? How? This made no sense.

When a few more snowflakes found their way down, Petulia finally noticed them as well. "What the...?" She held out her hand, catching one of the flakes. It melted immediately.

Miss Level stared up at the sky and saw a dark mass coming down. Her eyes widened. She pulled at Petulia's arm and started to run back to the cottage. Petulia was too confused to argue and just followed suit. The snow was coming down faster and heavier now. Finally, they reached the cottage, burst inside, and quickly pushed the door shut. A split second later and they would have been caught in a real snowstorm.

Petulia bent over in order to catch her breath. "What...is... going...on?"

Miss Level shook her head. "I don't know." She rubbed her arms to get some feeling back into them. Noticing how wet her clothes were, she turned to the gigantic oven and put a few blocks of wood in it. She pulled two kitchen chairs in front of the oven, then grabbed two more and put them next to the others.

"What are you doing?" asked Petulia.

"I am taking off these wet clothes and hanging them to dry in front of the oven." Miss Level unbuttoned her blouse and started to pull it out of her skirt waistband. "It will be the fastest way to get them dry and get us warm again." She hung her blouse over one of the chairs before kicking off her shoes and putting them in front of the oven as well.

Thinking she probably had a good point, Petulia joined her and started to undress as well.

A few minutes later both women were in their underwear, sitting in front of the oven, holding out their hands towards it for warmth.

"So," Miss Level began hesitantly, "does Melchior have powers to control the weather?"

Petulia stared into the oven fire. "Not that I know of, but apparently I didn't know him very well."

"No, I don't think it works like that," Miss Level mused. "If he could control the weather, you would have noticed something. Maybe a breeze when he was angry or something like that."

Petulia thought back over the years when they had been together. "No, nothing like that ever happened."

"Hmmm, that doesn't bring us any closer, then." Miss Level dropped her head into her right hand, resting her elbow on one knee. After a few minutes she said, "I can't think of anyone with that kind of power. Can you?"

"Well, there was this one witch that came to visit once," Petulia recollected. "She came over and had dinner with us. All during dinner, I could have sworn I felt a chill, but Melchior told me I was being silly. But there was this look in her eyes that just made me feel sure that she was doing something. I just couldn't tell what it was."

"That sounds promising." Miss Level perked right up. "Do you remember her name?"

"Yes, I do." Petulia blushed. "I just really hated her for messing with me like that." She shifted uneasily in her chair. "Her name was Austencia."

"Austencia? Are you sure?" Miss Level cocked her head at her friend, who glared back at her and nodded. "Well, there can't be too many of them around. Let me check something." She stood up and walked into the study, checking every book on the history shelf until she found the one she was looking for. Then she went back to the kitchen and sat down. "Now, let's see…"

"What is that?" Petulia tried to read the title of the book.

"Oh." Miss Level showed her the cover. "It's *The Genealogy of Witches.*"

"You have a book with the genealogy of witches?" Petulia asked incredulously.

"Yes, don't you?" Miss Level turned to the first page and scanned the family tree represented there.

"No." Petulia moved closer to see what Miss Level was doing. "So, how many witches are in that book?"

"All of them."

"*All* of them?" Petulia was – not for the first time – wondering if this woman in front of her was serious.

"Yes, all of them. It updates every time a new witch is born." Miss Level looked up and smiled at Petulia. "Once, I even saw it grow a new page."

"How is that possible?"

"Don't know." Miss Level looked back down and continued searching. "It must have been a great spell."

At that very moment, the book started to shake uncontrollably.

At once, Miss Level released it. "Speaking of which, I guess a new witch was just born."

They watched as the book lifted up in the air and turned round and round. The pages fluttered until the book found the right page. A flash of white light exploded from the book, right before it thumped back down onto Miss Level's lap.

"Umph."

"That's it? That's an update?" Petulia watched the book warily, thinking that it might do the same thing again at any moment (which was actually quite possible).

"Oh no." Miss Level bent closer to the open page.

"What?"

Miss Level just pointed at the page. So Petulia leaned in closer, scanning it until she found exactly what Miss Level was pointing at.

"Oh no."

"It could be a coincidence, but I don't really believe in those." Miss Level closed the book. There was no point in looking any further, as Austencia's name had just been eliminated from the page by a black mark.

"What does that mean?" Petulia asked the question, although she was quite sure she already knew the answer.

"She died." Miss Level rose from her chair again to put the book back on the shelf in the study.

"I guess I knew that." Petulia stood up too, and crossed to the kitchen window. She opened the curtain. "The snow has stopped."

"That makes sense, if it was her doing." Miss Level disappeared into the study. When she reappeared, she said, "I wonder why she would first cause it to snow if she was going to die?"

"Maybe she wanted to leave this world on a high note?"

Miss Level sat back down on her chair. Feeling a little chilly, she put her hands out to the fire again, even though she was quite sure that fire wouldn't be able to fix this chill. The women were quiet for a little while, both thinking quite similar things.

It was Miss Level who spoke first. "Or maybe she was forced to?"

"I was thinking the same thing." Petulia was still standing near the window, gazing out at the snow-covered forest. She didn't want to think this, but she couldn't help it. It was like her new friend had just said: it could be a coincidence. But Petulia didn't believe in coincidences either. She sighed and sat back down in front of the fire, imitating Miss Level's pose. Then she shook her head to clear her thoughts before inhaling deeply. "So, *if* Melchior did what we think he did, there is just one question. Why?" She looked at her companion. "What is the use of making it snow so hard? Nobody could see a damn thing, and everyone hurried back inside."

"I think you just answered your own question," Miss Level deadpanned.

At that moment, a low grumble resounded through the kitchen. Both women started.

"What was that?" Petulia asked.

"I don't know." Miss Level's eyes darted all over the place, not spotting anything.

Another grumble, a little louder this time.

"It sounds like it's coming from our feet." Then Miss Level looked down and yelled.

God's face was sticking out of a puddle of melted snow on the floor. He yelled back at her.

"What are you doing there?" Miss Level crossed her legs and scooted her chair back while Petulia jumped up to stand behind her own chair.

"Do you think this is nice for me? I thought I was going to be in one of your teas or something. This was not the view I had in mind." God shuddered.

"Well, let's not dwell on it," Miss Level muttered shyly.

"No, let's not." God raised his chin, which was quite a feat given that his head was coming out of a puddle on the floor. "I have some news about Melchior."

"What?" It was the first time Petulia had spoken since God's face had appeared.

God startled and stammered, "Oh, uhm, Petulia. I didn't see you there."

"Damn it, just tell us what you know." Petulia did not have the patience for this. Somehow, she still hoped she was wrong about Melchior.

Affronted, God turned back to Miss Level. At least she knew how to treat a wizard. "I scried for him again and he popped up in our world about an hour ago."

Miss Level looked at Petulia. "That is about the same time it started snowing."

"Yes, well," God continued, "he also popped back out of our world about five minutes ago."

"That's—" Miss Level began, but she was interrupted by God.

"When the snow stopped." He rolled his eyes. "Yes, I know."

"Not what I was going to say," Miss Level mumbled.

"Look," – God became slightly impatient – "casting a snow spell doesn't make him an evil man. It just means he has more powers than I knew about."

Miss Level swallowed loudly. "Well, we also have some news for you." She hesitated.

"Yes?" God's impatience was growing.

"He doesn't have that kind of power. Petulia would have known if he did." Miss Level swallowed again, uncertain as to whether she really wanted to say the next words out loud. "However, a witch he knew *does* have that power." A short glance at Petulia. "Or did. But she died...about five minutes ago."

The head in the puddle turned from Miss Level to Petulia and back again. "How do you know that?"

"Because I have a *Genealogy of Witches* and it updated while we were looking for her name."

"What is her name? I will check it myself." God glared at Miss Level.

"Austencia."

"That's it? No last name?"

Miss Level glared back at him. "How many Austencias do you know?"

"Fine." The head in the puddle dissolved.

Petulia leaned a bit closer over the empty puddle. "Is he gone? Can we sit down again?"

"I wouldn't just yet if I were you."

Petulia straightened back up, putting her hands on her waist. "Damn it."

God's head re-emerged from the puddle. The look on his face was solemn. "You are right. And this happened at the exact moment when the snow stopped?"

"Yes." Miss Level scooted just a little closer. "What do you think? I mean, we know what *we* think, but what do *you* think?"

God looked her straight in the eyes. "I think I am thinking the exact same thing you are."

Petulia rolled her eyes. "Damn it. Just come out with it." She stepped closer as well, making sure her underskirt didn't hover too close to his face. "Do you think Melchior had something to do with this?"

"It is too spooky to be a coincidence."

"That is what we thought as well." Miss Level sat up straighter. "So, what do we do now?"

Petulia glanced through the kitchen window. "I don't know about God here, but we can't do a damn thing. We are completely snowed in."

The head vanished from the puddle for a few seconds before reappearing. "Yes, I am snowed in as well."

Miss Level cocked her head. "With Austencia dead, the sun will most likely come out again really soon. So, we shouldn't be snowed in for too long. How about we wait it out for a day and try to think of a plan while we are stuck inside?"

"Sounds good," Petulia agreed.

"All right by me," God replied.

"Maybe we should also think about who else we might want to inform." Miss Level looked at the head in the puddle. "We don't want anyone else to get hurt because Melchior wants to use them, do we? And I think we will probably need a few more witches and wizards if we are going to stop him."

Grudgingly, God agreed to the plan: he would reappear in a day, this time in a bowl that would remain filled with water at all times, and they would discuss whatever plan they came up with. With that settled, his face disappeared from the puddle again.

Petulia stepped closer. "Is it safe?" She gazed at the puddle.

"Hang on." Miss Level grabbed the dishcloth and wiped up the melted snow. "There. No more puddle at our feet. It should be fine."

Both women sat back down and started to think of a plan and the people they wanted on their side.

*

A day later, God's face showed up in the bowl on the kitchen table. Miss Level and Petulia were sitting at the table, drinking tea and eating biscuits, so they weren't as startled this time.

"Are you still snowed in?" God's voice grumbled.

"Hello to you too," Miss Level replied. She said nothing else and just smiled at him.

He sighed. "Fine. Yes. Hello. Now, are you still snowed in?"

Petulia rolled her eyes at the two of them and sighed as well. "Yes, we are. Are you?"

"Yes." God glared at Miss Level. "I thought you said the sun would soon melt this stuff away."

She shrugged. "I guess the snow from the spell Austencia cast is tougher than ordinary snow."

God took a deep breath to begin a tirade against Miss Level, but Petulia cut him off. "Damn it, we are not here to discuss the weather, no matter how awful it is." She glared at him. "Have you found out anything more about why Melchior was here and what he was up to?"

God sulked. "No."

"We couldn't think of anything either." Petulia sipped from her cup.

All of a sudden, Miss Level smacked herself on the forehead. "Oh, I am so stupid." She rose quickly and went to the study. When she came back, she was holding a piece of parchment. "We should check *The Arcane News*."

"The what?" Petulia and God asked in unison.

"*The Arcane News*," Miss Level repeated, as if the name in itself were a perfect explanation.

"Yes, we understood what you said," Petulia replied testily, "but what is it?"

"Oh, I thought you knew. *The Arcane News* is a newsletter you can subscribe to. It gives you all the latest news in the world of mystery and witchcraft. Although I have to admit that some of their articles are somewhat ridiculous." Miss Level shook her head. "As if people are really interested in reading about some crop that looks like the head of King Edmund."

Petulia took a deep breath, trying to control her temper and not shout at Miss Level. "So, why would we want to read this *Arcane News* right now?"

"Well, if anything weird happens, it usually shows up in here. The explanation given isn't always correct, but it's a great source to find out what's happening." Miss Level started to read the piece of parchment.

Leaving her to it, Petulia turned to God's face in the bowl. "Have you thought about people you want to tell about Melchior?"

"The Briar sisters are on my list, although I don't really like them." His lip curled.

"Why is that?" Petulia sipped her tea.

"They always think they know best. Just because they are natural witches."

Petulia frowned. "*Natural* witches?" Wow, she really didn't know that much about magic.

"Yes, you know: born with magic, never had to study or anything. Although they did go to the Academy, but that was just to annoy all the other students who did have to work at it."

God's voice grew louder as his anger rose. "It doesn't make the others less than them, you know." His nostrils flared.

"All right." Petulia frowned again. "So why do you want them on our side then?"

"Because they are natural witches. Obviously." God looked at her as if she was stupid.

Well, that was it, then. Petulia decided to stop talking to him while Miss Level was occupied. Obnoxious man. She sipped her tea again and ignored the head protruding from the bowl.

"Ah, this sounds interesting." Miss Level raised her hand to get their attention, though she'd already had it from the moment she'd said 'ah'. "Yesterday, a guard of the wall at Edmundtown saw a dark figure walking around the wall's circumference, but at that time it was snowing so hard he couldn't make out who or what it was. He describes it as a floating, dark figure that was behaving erratically. It kept moving from one side to the other. He also heard a low howling sound which at first made him think it was a wolf, but as it got closer it got a lot bigger and he decided it couldn't possibly be a wolf."

The silence that followed was deafening.

"Why is that interesting?" God asked, giving Miss Level the benefit of the doubt because she had always been a little weird, but not stupid.

Miss Level looked up at Petulia, and then down at God's face in the bowl. "Isn't it obvious? Melchior did some kind of spell while it was snowing so that nobody would be outside to see him. The howling was probably a spell chant."

"If it *was* Melchior." Petulia wasn't so sure. "It might have been someone that got lost in the snow and was trying to get back inside the city walls."

"Then that person would have kept coming closer. But it says here…hang on…ah, here… 'And then the figure disappeared and the howling with it, just before it stopped snowing.'" Expectantly, Miss Level looked at her companions. "See?"

"It could have been him, I suppose," God conceded. "But what was he doing?"

"That is what we have to go and find out." Miss Level slid the piece of parchment across to the side of the table. "I suggest we meet up at the north wall – because that is where the figure was standing – as soon as the snow has melted enough for us to leave our homes and travel."

A deep sigh resounded from the bowl. "Fine. It is the first lead we have, so we might as well. Do you want me to inform the Briar sisters too?"

"Why would I want you to do that?" Miss Level frowned. "I hate them. I thought you did too."

"I do, but they are natural witches. We might want their powers on our side."

This time, it was Miss Level who conceded. "Fine. Check in with us tomorrow, around the same time, to see if we can travel."

"All right. See you tomorrow." And with those words, God's face disappeared from the bowl.

"Stupid Briar sisters," Miss Level muttered. "Bully sisters is more like it."

Petulia raised one eyebrow. "I take it you don't really like them."

"Whatever gave you that idea?" Miss Level stood up and took the parchment back into the study.

"Nothing," Petulia replied. "Absolutely nothing."

Twelve

The Witches' Guild

After paying Milly for their food and drinks, Petulia, Miss Level and Tobias leave the tavern and continue their journey. Petulia is still not sure they are doing the right thing by going to the Guild, but she knows better than to argue with Miss Level.

About half an hour later, they arrive at the South Gate of Clariceville. A very stoical guard stands watch. He immediately recognises Miss Level and greets her warmly.

"Hello, Miss Level. Gabriel not with you today?"

She smiles at him. "Afraid not, Walter. But he is at home if you want to go over after your shift."

"I just might. I have some great new ideas for our a cappella group." Walter beams.

"I am sure he would be happy to hear them."

Petulia, who is already dreading their visit to the Guild and just wants it over with, is in no mood for small talk. She pokes Miss Level in order to get her to hurry up.

Message understood, Miss Level says, "Well, we are just going to see the Guild for a spell."

Walter laughs hard and loud. "For a spell. Classic." He wipes a tear from his eye. "Anything I should worry about?"

Miss Level doesn't want to frighten him; after all, they could still be wrong. "No, just renewing our membership."

He stands aside and lets them pass. "All right, then. Have a nice day."

As soon as they enter the city, Petulia remarks, "I liked Gerald better."

Miss Level frowns at her. "You did? He was completely deaf and never remembered who you were. Who anybody was, for that matter."

"Well, I still liked him better."

Miss Level shrugs and walks on.

Neither woman notices that Tobias has doubled over next to them. When they hear him vomiting, they finally pay attention.

"Oh dear," Miss Level says. She goes to his side and softly rubs his back as he continues to throw up. "You get used to the smell. You do. It used to be a lot worse. At least they have started to make up some rules, like, 'No throwing the contents of the chamber pot out into the street.' That was a real improvement."

Tobias motions for her to please stop talking because it is only making things worse. A chamber pot is what he thinks it is, isn't it?

In the meantime, Petulia goes into a nearby shop and buys a handkerchief. She sprinkles a bit of lavender oil on it and passes it to Tobias. "Here, keep this in front of your nose. It will help."

Tobias happily accepts the handkerchief and does as instructed. Big improvement.

"Everybody ready?" Petulia asks. Without waiting for an answer, she walks on, expecting the others to simply follow her, which of course they do.

It is a good thing that they entered through the South Gate. This means the Guild's headquarters isn't too far away to walk.

The Witches' Guild headquarters is an unremarkable building with dark grey bricks and wooden shutters. At least, that is how it appears. Unfortunately, this is just a glamour that the Head Master maintains on the building. If people could see the real building, they would be amazed at how decrepit it really is. Roof tiles and pieces of brick keep falling to the ground. It won't be too long before one hits a passer-by. But until then, the Head Master will stick to his plan and keep the glamour in place. It costs a lot less to make the place look tidy than to actually fix it. He is a very cheap and stingy man.

Whenever Miss Level enters the building, she feels ill at ease, worried that some day something might fall on top of her head. So, without telling anyone, each time she visits the place, she fixes small things. It started with mirrors, chandeliers, windows, a cross-beam – basically, anything that had the potential to fall on her head. She has been doing this for so many years that the upper part of each room – starting from one metre and a half up the walls, and including the ceiling – looks exquisite compared to the bottom part. It is a miracle that nobody has noticed. So far, Miss Level is the only one who can see it. The rest see only the Head Master's glamour, but still, in a house full of witches, not one? The problem is that everyone is used to the glamour.

They already know why it is there, so why bother to see what is underneath? They have no reason to believe that anything has changed. Otherwise, the glamour would have been lifted, right?

When Tobias enters the building, his gaze slips from the ceiling to the floor. "Why does it look so weird?"

"It is a glamour. You might experience a bit of dizziness because the picture appears to move constantly, but you will get used to it." Petulia doesn't even look at him when she replies.

He is still looking up and down. "All right. But why only do half of the room?"

"What?" Petulia looks around as if seeing everything for the first time. Slowly, the glamour dissolves before her eyes and she can see the half-finished building. "So, he finally decided to do the repairs. Do you think he came into some money recently?" She looks down at her friend, who is blushing so hard she looks like a strawberry with legs. "You didn't!"

"I couldn't stand it any more!" Miss Level exclaims. "The other day, plaster from the ceiling nearly hit Euphagia in the head! I didn't want to be the next victim!"

Petulia looks around again. "How long have you been doing this?"

"About a hundred years. Just small bits here and there." Miss Level glances around as well. "I guess I visit the place more often than I thought."

"I guess you do."

The three of them are still staring at the ceiling when the Head Master walks into the Great Hall. He startles – he hadn't been expecting any visitors – but recovers quickly.

"Miss Level, always a nice surprise to see you." He shakes her hand warmly in both of his own. Then he glances at the person next to her. "And who is this?" He grabs Tobias's hand and shakes it fervently.

"My name is Tobias," Tobias says, trying to get his hand back.

The Head Master's gaze slides over to the third visitor and all the warmth disappears from his voice and his eyes. "Petulia." Ice cold. "I had hoped we would never see you again."

"I can assure you, Dirk, the feeling is quite mutual."

The mere mention of his first name sends a violent nervous twitch to the Head Master's left eye. Of course, Petulia knew it would. A smirk appears on her face.

"Well, you haven't changed a bit." He slaps his hand over his eye and turns back to Miss Level. "I suppose you had no other choice than to bring her. Did you?"

"Not really, no," is the reply.

The Head Master – Dirk – sighs. "Very well, then. Let us go to my office."

He leads the way up the stairs to the left wing of the building. The trio quietly follow. The two women already know the way and don't pay any attention to their surroundings, but Tobias really takes in all the details. It is a little confusing with the contrast between the decrepit bits and the renovated ones, and the fact that the border between those two states is horizontal doesn't make it any easier. Eventually they arrive at Dirk's office. He opens the door and lets them in. The first thing the three of them notice is that nothing in this room is even slightly repaired.

"Huh," Miss Level mumbles. "I guess I never go into this room."

Petulia leans in a bit and replies, "Clearly."

Dirk goes behind his desk and sits down. "Please, do sit down." He motions them to the available chairs.

There are only two of them, so Tobias quickly says, "I will keep standing. I like standing."

"Damn it," Petulia mutters.

She and Miss Level step up to the chairs. They are so crooked that it seems a dangerous enterprise to actually sit on them. Cautiously, they lower themselves into the seats. An ominous creaking resounds, but the chairs hold fast. As long as they don't move about, the chairs will most likely hold out.

Dirk heaves a heavy sigh of disappointment. "The glamour doesn't work on you three, does it?"

"Not really, no." Miss Level feels sorry for him.

He scrubs his hand across his face. "I know. It is a mess." He regards Miss Level gratefully. "And I really appreciate the small fixes you have performed in the past. I try to do the same but there is always some emergency that needs my immediate attention and absorbs all my energy and magic." He pauses, and then suddenly sits up straight. "Anyway, you didn't come by to hear me whine, did you?"

"Not really, no," Miss Level repeats.

"So how may I help you?" Dirk smiles at them expectantly.

"To be perfectly honest, we have an emergency that will require all your energy and magic," Miss Level says apologetically.

Another big sigh. "I figured as much. I am pretty sure she," – pointing at Petulia – "wouldn't be here otherwise."

"You are right, I wouldn't, so take this seriously and stop complaining." Petulia is already fed up with the man. Patience is not one of her virtues.

"Fine. What is it?"

The two women look at Tobias, who has been almost invisible until now. He looks back at them in confusion. Do they expect *him* to explain everything? He doesn't think he's qualified for that.

"Go on," Petulia says. "Show him your stick."

"Oh." Tobias is relieved. He pulls the stick out of his back pocket and puts it on the desk.

Immediately, Dirk rolls back his desk chair. "Is that what I think it is?"

In unison, "Yes."

"Has either one of you touched it?" He directs this question at Petulia and Miss Level.

"Yes," Miss Level says.

"Petulia?"

"Yes."

Tobias feels like he is back in high school and being chided for not doing his homework. He also feels that Petulia is being blamed for something she didn't do. "To be fair, it wasn't her fault. I pushed it at her faster than she could get away from it."

Dirk doesn't look like he believes that, but he nods nonetheless. "I understand." He scrubs his hand across his face again. "So, the message was sent."

"Yes," Miss Level says once again.

Dirk looks straight at Tobias and narrows his eyes. "How did you get this stick?"

The young man shrugs. "I found it on the street. It looked interesting, so I picked it up."

"Then what happened?"

Tobias hesitates. "I twirled it and opened a kind of portal."

Dirk's eyes widen. "And you just stepped through it?"

Another shrug.

"Not knowing what to expect?"

Yet another shrug.

"Where did you go?"

Tobias glances at the two women, knowing very well that he hasn't told them the full story. "Well, first I stepped into a desert but it was too damn hot, so I twirled the stick again and then I was in a forest."

Dirk looks at the women. "I understand why the portal opened up in the forest, but any idea which desert it might have been?"

Petulia scratches her chin, while Miss Level gazes up at the ceiling, hoping that the answer might lie there. No such luck.

Miss Level turns to Tobias. "Were there any specific markers? Any landmarks?"

"No, just a lot of sand and a lot of heat. To be completely honest, I didn't stay that long."

"Petulia? Do you think it might be possible to go back there?"

Petulia thinks about it for a while. "Well, only Tobias has seen the desert. Maybe if he used that stick, he would be able to open another portal to it." She shifts her gaze to the young man. "You would have to focus your attention really hard."

Tobias figures it can't be much harder than conjuring up his mom's stew. "I think I could manage it."

The Head Master chimes in. "It could be very dangerous, young man. Do not underestimate it."

"I said I could do it and I will."

"Fine," Dirk says. "Let me just get some things and we can be on our way."

In unison, the others ask, "*You* are coming?"

"Of course I am." And with those words, he steps into an adjoining room and starts rummaging through his closet. He has noticed before that people tend to speak in unison when they are around him and he is nervous. It has happened twice already with these three. Maybe it is his special gift? It is general knowledge that each witch or wizard has a special gift that they might not be aware of. Is this his? If it is, a lot of good it will do him. It isn't really something with which one can defend oneself, or anything like that. He supposes it could make things easier when his hearing starts to fade and he has trouble understanding people. He shakes his head, grabs what he needs, and heads back into his office. No use thinking about that any further, is it?

While he was packing, Petulia and Miss Level had an entire conversation using only facial expressions. The gist of it was Petulia expressing her concerns about Dirk joining their quest and Miss Level telling her to be nice. When Dirk returns, he feels a weird tension in the room. He wonders if it has anything to do with him.

All doubt evaporates as soon as Petulia opens her mouth. "Doesn't the Guild need you to stay here? I mean, what is a guild without its Head Master?"

To be honest, she should have known that this question would only have the opposite effect to the one she desires.

"You don't really expect me to leave the three of you in charge of this mission, do you? Need I remind you of what happened the last time you were in charge of a mission? I do believe it is that which we intend to fix now, is it not?" Dirk smirks.

Petulia points her finger at him. "Last time was not my fault. And you know it."

Sensing that this could get out of hand very quickly, Miss Level jumps in. "Now, now. Let bygones be bygones." She holds out her hands at both of them as if to ensure a certain distance between them. "Head Master, please do join us. We could use your expertise." When nothing else seems to happen, she continues, "Why don't we go now? The sooner we get this over with, the sooner we can part ways again."

Dirk turns to her with a smile. "A wise suggestion. Let's go."

Petulia just snorts and follows them. Tobias feels a bit left out, but joins them as well. They need him, anyway. He is the one with the stick.

After a lengthy debate between Petulia and the Head Master, they decide to go back to the forest and open the portal there, just in case it backfires. They trudge through the trees and away from the path until they find a somewhat sheltered spot that appears to be good enough.

"All right," Petulia says, "let's see what you've got."

Tobias figures that this is his cue. He pulls the stick from his back pocket. Then he closes his eyes, concentrating on the desert that he saw the first time he went through the portal. When he feels that he can't focus any more than he already is doing, he starts to twirl the stick. Slowly, a portal opens up. Petulia, Miss Level and Dirk are astonished at his level of competence, mainly because they figured he had no magical background.

"Good." Petulia takes charge before Dirk can. "Let's hold hands and walk through." She looks pointedly at Tobias. "You are going last so you can grab the stick before the portal closes." She squints her eyes. "But I bet you already knew that."

She holds out her hands to Dirk and Miss Level, then motions to Tobias to hold Miss Level's other hand. This way, the Head Master will be the first to go through the portal, just in case a horrible beast awaits them. Dirk himself only sees it as a compliment that he has been selected to lead the mission. He inhales deeply, sticks out his chest, and moves forward.

Right before she goes through the portal, Miss Level remembers that they have forgotten one thing: Tobias hasn't yet learned to focus his energy on only doing what he wants it to do. She can just see a ripple shoot up into the air before the portal closes behind him, holding his stick.

He can feel another hit of magic. "Wonderful."

Why have they done this? Surely, the witch who touched the stick would know not to?

How much time has passed? Have they forgotten about him? If they have, he will soon make them remember.

A small crack appears in the bark of the tree. "Beautiful."

All of a sudden, he senses that the stick is no longer nearby. It has disappeared altogether. "Noooooooo!" Enraged, he starts picking at the crack in the bark.

Thirteen

Desert Plains and Dunes

Petulia, Miss Level, Dirk and Tobias find themselves standing in the sweltering heat of a desert plain.

"Now do you understand why I didn't stay long enough the last time to take in my surroundings?" Tobias asks.

The other three just nod, too hot to say a word at first.

The Head Master opens up the bag he brought and hands out four water bottles.

"Good thinking, Dirk," says Petulia, which immediately makes him take back her bottle. As you have probably already noticed, Petulia is the stubborn kind of witch. So, instead of apologising, she conjures up her own bottle of water, enriched with vitamins and flavoured with orange. That ought to teach him.

The only response Miss Level can give to any of this is to roll her eyes and walk over to one of the dunes surrounding them. Slowly, she trudges up it. The sand shifts under her feet, making it very hard to move forward. The other three try to follow her as best they can.

When Miss Level reaches the top, she stops and looks around. In the distance she can see a shimmer, just as Petulia reaches her. Something is reflecting the sun. Unfortunately, it is located in the direction from which they have just come.

"Damn it," – Petulia puffs – "you picked the wrong dune. We should have gone the other way."

"I didn't pick the wrong dune – I picked the biggest one so that I could see everything, and it worked." Miss Level kneels down and tucks the back of her skirt underneath her legs. Then she lifts up the edge of her skirt in front of her and pushes off. She slides all the way to the bottom of the dune, leaving her gaping companions behind. When she reaches the bottom, she stands up and brushes the sand from her clothes. Then she looks up to see what is keeping the rest of them.

At once Petulia copies her friend and slides down the sandy slope. The two men sigh. They try to be graceful in following the women, but fail utterly. Both of them fall quite quickly and roll down the dune.

When everyone is gathered back together, they set out to hurdle the next dune. It takes even more time than the first one. Finally reaching the top, they can see that they need to pass at least three more dunes before they will be even close to the source of the shimmer.

"This is stupid." Petulia doubles over, nearly landing face down in the sand. "We are witches. We shouldn't have to walk."

Out of breath, Miss Level replies, "I know, but I left the two-seater broom in the forest and there are no branches here to make a new one."

Dirk and Tobias look at them quizzically, having absolutely no idea what they are talking about.

Then Dirk shakes his head. "Wait a minute." He puts his bag down and rummages through it. After five minutes, he stands back up with a small vial in his hand. "I knew I brought this."

"Is that what I think it is?" Petulia asks.

Dirk shrugs. "Blueblossom owed me a favour."

"Blueblossom?" Tobias interjects. "That's a weird name."

"Not for a fairy," Dirk answers. "Blueblossom is the night guard at the fairy factory."

"And the fairy factory is…what exactly?"

"That's where they make fairy dust." Dirk shakes the vial in front of Tobias's face.

"And fairy dust does what?"

"It has a lot of magical uses." Dirk shrugs.

Tobias smiles, as if in on a secret. "It can make you fly?"

"Yes." Dirk beams. "It can definitely make you fly." He takes a bit of dust out of the vial and blows it over Miss Level, Petulia and Tobias. "But remember, it only lasts for eighteen hours." Then he sprinkles some on himself and puts the vial back in his bag.

"So how does this work? Do I need to think happy thoughts?"

Dirk cocks his head. "I suppose you could, but I don't think it will make you fly better."

Miss Level has had quite enough of this conversation. "Tobias, just focus on flying and where you want to go." She gently lifts up into the air. "See?"

Sure, he thinks, that explains it. He closes his eyes and thinks of flying. Nothing happens. He thinks of floating through the sky. Nothing. Envisioning himself as Superman doesn't help either. He opens his eyes and sees the others hovering above him, waiting for him to join them. He closes his eyes again. Maybe if he thinks about where he wants to go. Get me to the shimmer?

Suddenly, a slight breeze blows across his face. He opens his eyes again and finds himself standing outside a tent. Where are the others?

In the blink of an eye and from out of thin air, they appear before him.

Dirk shrugs apologetically. "We completely forgot that that was also an option."

Annoyed at how slowly this is going, he pokes one finger through the small hole in the bark of the tree. That is how far he has got. If only he had his magic, but over the years it has slipped away from him. Magic only sticks around when you use it. Even the small bits he collected from the ripples are already drained. He needs to figure out how to get his magic back. The stick will help immensely.

He starts scratching away at the bark again. He will so need a manicure after this.

Fourteen

Weird Names

Tobias looks at the tent standing next to them. He soon realises what caused the shimmer they saw: a giant satellite dish is strapped to the top of the mast that is peeking through the roof of the tent. Dirk, Petulia and Miss Level follow his gaze. The three of them cock their heads to the left. A funny sight.

"What is that?" Dirk has no idea what to make of it.

"I don't know," Miss Level says, "but I have seen something like it before." She turns to Petulia. "Remember last year when we kept going to that theatre to create men for Princess Clarice?"

Dirk's head snaps towards her. "That was you?" His eyes widen.

Petulia's eyes narrow. "Yes, that was us. Why?"

"Nothing," Dirk replies innocently. "Nothing at all."

Petulia puts her hands on her hips. "What is it? What aren't you saying?"

"Nothing," Dirk repeats. "I just didn't know that that was your work. It was good. Some first-class creations, if you ask me."

Petulia, astonished at how much that compliment means to her, says gruffly, "Well, nobody asked you." She turns to Miss Level in order to smoothly change the subject. "Yes, of course I remember that. Why?"

"Well, there were discs like that on some of the roofs in that city." Miss Level gazes at her friend. "You didn't see them?"

Petulia just shakes her head.

Tobias asks, "None of you know what that is?"

Three heads shake.

Tobias looks up again. "I guess that means we are in my world now. I wonder where exactly?"

At that moment, they hear a voice coming closer to them. Not really having anywhere to go, they wait patiently for it to round the corner of the tent and meet them. Closer and closer it comes. Tobias tries to discern what language is being spoken. Maybe he can figure out if the voice is friend or foe before they actually meet. The closer the voice comes, the more words he is able to understand. Definitely English, then. Good thing too, because that is all he speaks.

A foot appears, quickly followed by the rest of the body of a paunchy man, dressed in khaki, and wearing a silly hat to cover his balding head. Right behind him is a slim woman, also dressed in khaki with a hat. They stop abruptly. Clearly, they were not expecting to find someone standing here, let alone four someones.

"Who the bloody hell are you?" The man reaches behind his back and pulls out a rifle.

Immediately, Tobias raises his hands to the sky. "Please. Don't shoot."

The other three swiftly follow his example.

"Are you trying to steal our camels?" the man asks.

"We wouldn't dare," Tobias says.

At the same time, Dirk replies, "Why would we? We can fly."

The man cocks the gun. "Where did you come from?"

"Well," Tobias says, "that is actually a difficult question to answer."

The gun is raised to take aim. "Try it."

"Right." And then the babbling starts. Tobias can't stop himself. "I'm originally from Kansas, and that is where I was yesterday when I found this stick that can open portals. The first portal opened here but it was too hot, so I quickly left. The second one opened in a beautiful forest, so I walked around, testing out what else the stick could do." Deep breath. "That is when I met these lovely ladies, who warned me not to do that and took me to see this guy so that we could help prevent catastrophe from happening, which somehow brought us here—"

Petulia slaps the back of his head to snap him out of his ramblings.

"Ow. Thank you." Tobias squeezes his mouth shut to stop himself saying anything else. Why didn't he just say, 'Looking for some water, do you have any?'

The khaki-clad woman puts her hand on the man's trigger-happy arm. "I think they are delusional. God knows how long they have gone without water."

The man lowers the gun. "You are probably right. They look completely harmless, anyway. Look at them, shivering like bloody cowards."

"Why don't you go get the supplies, like we were doing before we stumbled upon them?"

"Great idea, love." He kisses her, and off he goes.

"Please." The woman gestures for them to follow her. "Come inside."

Not really knowing what else to do, they follow her around the corner and she opens a flap of the tent to let them in. The inside is luxuriously decorated with rich colours and Middle Eastern style. Cushions lie everywhere. She motions to some of them, which are placed around a small table. Suddenly, the four companions feel exhausted. They flop down on the cushions.

The woman takes glasses from a cupboard and fills them with water from a crystal carafe. "Before I give you anything to drink, please introduce yourselves."

"Of course." Feeling a little guilty that he didn't think of that before, Tobias goes first. "I am Tobias."

"The man from Kansas." The woman smiles at him and hands him a glass.

"My name is Petulia." She also receives a glass of water.

"I am Miss Level."

"No first name?" the woman asks as she hands over another glass.

"Not one I'm sharing," Miss Level answers coyly.

"Fair enough." The woman turns to the Head Master. "And you?"

"My name is Dirk."

The water Petulia has just sipped spurts from her mouth.

"This is not true?" the woman asks.

"No, I mean, yes, it is." Petulia wipes her mouth with the back of her hand. "I just can't get used to hearing it. Does he look like a Dirk to you?"

"I guess not, but you can't choose the name your parents give you, can you?" The woman smiles at Dirk and hands him the last glass of water. "And on that note, my name is Elizabella. I guess my parents couldn't decide between Elizabeth and Isabella, so they mixed and matched. I have grown to like it."

That seems to cheer him up quite a bit. He thanks Elizabella for the glass of water and drinks greedily.

Just at that moment, the man with the rifle steps into the tent. He is carrying a large box, which he promptly drops on the floor. "Bloody hell. That is heavy."

"Careful, darling. Something might break."

The man takes off his hat, revealing more of his balding grey head. He wipes the sweat off his brow and regards the guests sitting at his coffee table. "So who do we have here?"

Elizabella introduces everyone. "This is Tobias, the man from Kansas. Petulia and Miss Level. And this one is Dirk."

"You've got quite well acquainted, haven't you?" The man walks over to the cupboard, takes out a glass for himself, and fills it with water from the carafe. Then he walks over to the table and flops down. "Well, then, I am Adelbert."

"We've got the weird name thing in common," Elizabella says proudly. "Among other things, of course."

Dirk is intrigued. "What else do you have in common?"

Elizabella sits down gracefully on one of the cushions, removing her own hat, and in the process releasing a cascade of auburn hair. "Well, archaeology, for one thing. We both got into the field because of *Indiana Jones*. But the best thing we have in common is that we both adore Melchior." Met with astonished looks on the faces of her guests, she elaborates. "You know Melchior, right? One of the wise men who brought gifts to the baby Jesus?"

The four of them just nod.

"He brought gold with him, which is all right, I guess." Elizabella leans in closer. "But we have learned that he became fascinated with the gift from Balthazar: myrrh. Nobody else really understood its medicinal qualities, but he did."

In unison, the four reply, "Of course."

"And this is the best part: we have combined our love of archaeology with our love for Melchior. See, nobody really knows where he came from. It doesn't really say in the Bible – there's just a small reference to him coming from the East. But we have figured it out. We are on the cusp of a great discovery." Elizabella points to the north. "Right beyond the ridge there are some ruins that we are exploring. We are positive that we have found Melchior's home." She gazes lovingly at Adelbert.

"Bloody right, we have. It doesn't matter what those twats at the Jeffersonian think. Taking away our sponsorship like that. Complete idiots, that's what they are."

"We will prove them wrong soon enough, darling."

As the couple gaze dreamily into each other's eyes, all this information settles into Miss Level's brain. "Although I am not very well acquainted with Melchior, I would really like to see these ruins, if you don't mind?"

Everyone in the tent stares at her. Some with admiration, some with wonder, and one with absolute contempt.

"You must come with us tomorrow, then!" exclaims Elizabella. "It is too late now. The sun has just set, so the temperature will drop very soon." She pats Adelbert's arm. "Darling, will you start up the generator so we can have some heat in the tent?"

Tobias is flabbergasted. Are they not in the same tent as he is? Are they not sweating like pigs? He is! But as a bit more time passes by, he admits that the temperature has indeed dropped a lot, and he is grateful when the generator kicks in.

Fifteen

The Ruin

It has been a fitful night for Miss Level. She kept wondering what they were going to find the next day. It can't be a coincidence that the portal sent them here, to meet these lovely people who just happen to be obsessed with Melchior. If Elizabella and Adelbert find out that the ruins actually *are* Melchior's home, then they might also be in danger. They have no idea of the power of the wizard they're dealing with. They just think he was a kind old man who brought a gift to a baby. To be honest, Miss Level doesn't really understand why that has been deemed important. She has brought gifts to babies a dozen times, and nobody mentions her in the history books because of that. Maybe it was a special baby, like a King or something? Still, nobody remembers what Princess Clarice got when she was born. Well, actually they do: it was a horse which threw her off its back when she was four. Maybe that was an omen. The horse knew even back then that he didn't like her. And now everyone else knows that as well.

Anyway, Miss Level is getting way off track. Melchior, right. She wonders what he would think about them visiting his home.

She knows she wouldn't like it happening to her; at least when she wasn't there herself. That, of course, makes her think of Gabriel. Does he miss her? When she left the cottage she didn't really know how long she would be gone, and if they really are in a different world there's no way she can get a message to him.

It was thoughts like these that kept her up all night, so when Elizabella comes in to wake them, Miss Level is not in her usual cheerful mood. She is tired and cranky. She is Petulia…

Petulia, in turn, also had a fitful night. She kept wondering why Dirk paid her that compliment, and why she liked it. Something must be seriously wrong with her. But when their hostess comes to wake them, she feels remarkably cheerful. She has to stop this immediately or she will turn into Miss Level.

Tobias slept well. He dreamed about his stick and all the magic he could do with it. He just hopes that, after all is said and done about Melchior, he can keep the stick. Maybe he should ask his companions about that?

Dirk slept all right until about halfway through the night, when he thought he heard Petulia calling his name. He sat up and looked at her. She seemed to be sound asleep, mumbling a bit. He could have sworn that he heard his name. Could she be dreaming about him? After that, he lay awake for the rest of the night, wondering why he only gets the twitch in his eye when Petulia says his name. It never happens with anyone else. By the time Elizabella comes to wake them, he's decided that it's just because she irks him. That is all.

You can probably imagine how silent our companions are at the breakfast table. Nobody really notices because Elizabella and Adelbert talk constantly: about the dig, about their marriage (open), about their wedding (themed), about the funding they had and lost. It is only when they start to talk about Melchior that the others pay attention.

"No one has ever really thought about where he came from," Elizabella gazes lovingly at her spouse, "but we haven't done anything *but* think of that. And here we are."

Tobias interrupts. "Where exactly is 'here'?"

Elizabella looks at him quizzically. "You don't know where you are?"

"Not really, no."

"Did you just get dropped here?"

"Something like that."

"Is it a game?" She becomes very excited. "Are we on some kind of hidden-camera programme?"

Tobias quickly figures that it might speed things up if Elizabella and Adelbert think that. "Something like that." He is wrong.

"Are we even allowed to tell you where you are, then? I mean, we wouldn't want to break any rules, you know."

"Of course you are," Tobias improvises. "The object of the game is for us to get home, any way we can. But in order for us to do that, we kind of need to know where we are first." He smiles at their hosts.

"Of course!" Elizabella exclaims. "Well, we are in the Kalahari Desert."

"Huh, I never would have guessed that." Tobias is astounded. Africa? He is in Africa? Of course, he has just been in a completely different world, so perhaps Africa isn't that big of a leap after all.

"Does that help?"

"Yes, it does. Now I already know how to get back."

"How?"

Tobias smiles. "I can't tell you that. You will just have to watch the show."

Elizabella looks at her husband. "Oh, we will."

Trying to get back on topic, Miss Level asks, "So how did you figure out to come here?"

"Well, it was thought that Melchior was from the Middle East. But that was wrong. We found a depiction of the man that was made during his lifetime. In the background there is a certain type of tree that only grows in Africa. It is the tree where he got his myrrh from. When we narrowed it down further, we found that that specific tree could only be found near one small village." Elizabella pours herself some tea while taking a deep breath. "Well, we went there and asked around. Apparently, there is a folk tale in that village about a mysterious man who always came from the desert and visited the tree. So here we are."

"Wow, and now you say you have found some ruins?"

"Yes." Elizabella beams. "And they are exquisite." She blows on her tea. "As soon as I finish my tea, we will show you."

"Mind you," Adelbert says, "we have just started digging so we have only uncovered the top of the house so far. The rest is still covered in sand."

"But we can go inside, right?" Miss Level knows she sounds too eager, but she just had to ask.

"Yes, but only in a small part of the house." Adelbert starts to wonder if their guests are really who they say they are. Elizabella is too trusting for her own good. He should have just shot them the moment they met.

His wife, however, is as clueless as ever. "Oh, but you have to see it. There is a beautiful mural of a black tree in the greenest forest you have ever seen."

It can't be, can it? The four companions stare at each other. Can it?

After breakfast, they go outside. It isn't even seven o'clock yet but the heat is really starting to build.

Elizabella and Adelbert lead the way, walking just a bit faster than the others. Adelbert holds his wife's arm as he whispers, "I don't trust them. I mean, they don't even have any bloody luggage."

"Maybe that is part of the game?" she whispers back.

Behind them, there is also a lot of whispering going on.

"A mural of a black tree in a green forest?" Miss Level wonders. "How can that be?"

Dirk scratches his head, while Petulia replies, "He was very powerful. Maybe he had the power of foresight."

Still scratching, Dirk chimes in, "It is possible."

"But why didn't he do anything to stop it, then?"

"Maybe he wasn't that practised? Maybe he didn't know he was going to end up inside the tree?"

"Possible."

At that moment, they arrive at another tent. This one is a lot bigger than the one they just left. Elizabella and Adelbert are already waiting for them.

"What is this?" Tobias asks.

"We put a tent over the excavation," Elizabella explains. "Otherwise, all our work could be gone the next day. There are quite a lot of sandstorms in this area. I am pleasantly surprised that there wasn't one last night."

Little does she know that part of the reason there wasn't a sandstorm is standing in front of her. Weather anomalies don't like witches. Even raindrops don't fall on them. The sun has no problem with them whatsoever. So as per usual, the weather is really nice because there are witches around.

Adelbert holds the tent open for his wife and the others. When everyone is inside, he checks that the rifle is still strapped to his back, ready to go. He donned it right after breakfast, explaining that there might be some wild animals around. Elizabella looked at him funny but in the end she just shrugged it off. However, none of the others reacted in any way, even though everyone knows that animals don't come to this part of the desert. Something about strange vibes. Adelbert really doesn't trust these people...

When he enters the tent, he finds the five of them standing in a neat row, staring at the top of the sand-covered ruins.

"Beautiful, isn't it?" Elizabella says.

In unison, the four strangers answer, "Yes, it is." That is something else weird about them. They occasionally say stuff in unison. Something like that might happen once or twice, but this is already the seventh time. That is just wrong. Like they're mindless clones. But they look nothing alike.

Petulia casts an angry look at Dirk. If he does that unison crap one more time, she is going to strangle him. Dirk just shrugs back at her: it is a nervous habit he can't control.

"Shall we go inside?" Elizabella is eager to show them everything.

Petulia replies, before anyone else has the opportunity to even think something in unison, "We would love to."

"Great. Follow me." Slowly, Elizabella begins to climb up a sandy slope towards the top of the roof.

When they all reach the top, they see a hole in the roof. Looking through it, they stare right into an atrium with a small dried-up pool in the middle of it.

"We have already successfully cleared out all of the sand from this room, but the others are still chock-a-block full of sand and rocks." Elizabella walks a bit further to the side, where a ladder is waiting for them. "Only one person on the ladder at all times, please. I will go first and call out when the next person can come down." She swings her leg over the hole, finding a rung quite smoothly, and descends.

About a minute later, she calls out for the next person. Petulia steps up first. Her skirt makes it a bit harder to swing her leg, but she does quite well. Two minutes later, Elizabella calls out again.

This time, Miss Level steps up. "Tobias, I might just need your help." She tries valiantly to swing her leg over the side, but it is useless. She is a lot shorter than the two women who are already down there.

Tobias hastens to her and hesitantly grabs her under her arms, lifting her like a child over the side and indicating where she can find a rung to step on. When she finally finds it, she thanks him and slowly descends. It takes her five full minutes to reach the bottom; then Elizabella calls out again.

Tobias looks at Dirk. "Is it all right if I go next?"

"Of course, young man."

So, Tobias also swings his leg over, smoothly finding a rung, and races down. One minute later, there is another call from Elizabella.

Dirk takes a deep breath. He never told any of them that he's afraid of heights; mostly the idea of falling off them. He takes another deep breath and wills himself to step up to the ladder. Unwillingly, he gazes down and quickly steps backwards. He really shouldn't have done that.

Adelbert recognises the problem immediately. He steps up to the hole and shouts, "Go on, love. We are going to stay up here to make sure nothing happens."

A hesitant "All right" resounds.

"Thank you." Dirk nods at him.

"It is nothing. I have already seen it anyway." Adelbert smiles back, thinking that he might be able to get some answers out of this one.

Sixteen

Just Some Spring Cleaning

Elizabella turns around with a flashlight in her hand. "This is the central room. Gorgeous, isn't it?"

Miss Level, Petulia and Tobias look around in wonder. There are murals everywhere but the most prominent one is right in the middle of the largest wall: a big black tree standing in the middle of the greenest forest ever depicted.

"It looks so real," Miss Level mutters.

"Doesn't it?" Elizabella exclaims. "It is the best mural from that time that I have ever seen. So much detail." She pauses for a minute. "The other murals are also very nice, but this is definitely my favourite."

At the mention of the other murals, Petulia looks around the room. To the left of the big mural is a smaller one depicting Melchior surrounded by people who seem to view him as some kind of saviour. She supposes that he was to some people; mostly ones who suffered from arthritis. Myrrh is really good for that. She notices that the mural is cracked straight from the top left corner to the bottom right one. Then she moves over to the next mural and stops dead in her tracks. She stares at it, not quite registering what she is seeing but certain that she knows what it is.

Tobias joins her. "That woman looks like you."

Both of them gaze at the mural. They see a man kneeling in front of a woman, holding up his hands. The man is clearly Melchior.

Suddenly, it dawns on Tobias. "It was you," he whispers. "You are the woman he loved. The woman that turned him down."

"Hush," Petulia whispers back. "Don't say anything. We will talk about this later."

This is a lie, of course. She's always told people that she disliked Melchior and turned him down because of that. But it isn't really true. She's never told them about her relationship with Melchior and how she was in awe of him. He was her mentor, and she learned so much from him. He showed her things that were in between light and dark, and every time he performed a spell she saw a glint of hunger in his eyes. Once, she delighted in teetering on the edge herself. But she came to her senses and tried to get Melchior to do likewise, but it was too late. And then he went and proposed.

She had known that it would only take a small thing to send him fully into the world of dark magic. But she had also known that she could not marry him. That glint in his eyes had got worse and worse and she would not be able to make it disappear. When she said no, his eyes turned red with anger. Knowing that he was a very powerful wizard who had just been rejected, she turned and ran. Maybe she shouldn't have done that, but that red glow had promised indescribable pain. So she ran and ran…right into

Miss Level. Petulia glances over at her friend, who is standing on the other side of the chamber. That was the first time they met. She remembers the soft purple glow that surrounded Miss Level every time she got angry, and how it made her feel safe. Miss Level turned out to be the best friend anyone could ever have.

After a while, Petulia notices that Tobias has gone completely rigid beside her. She wonders what he will do with this new bit of information. He doesn't seem to be doing anything.

In silence, Tobias turns back to the mural, angry that the women didn't mention this vital piece of information about Petulia earlier. All of a sudden, he realises that this mural, like the previous one, is cracked straight from the top left corner to the bottom right. He looks around at the other murals. Every single one of them is cracked in the same way, except the one with the tree. How peculiar.

Petulia follows his gaze and notices the same thing. She looks at the images in detail and realises that all the cracked murals depict things that have already happened. Of course, Melchior being trapped in the tree has already happened as well, but maybe that mural isn't cracked because that event is still happening. Petulia sidles over to Miss Level, who is still standing in front of the tree mural with Elizabella. "It is strange that all the other murals are damaged, but not this one," she says to their host.

"You are quite right," Elizabella replies. "We haven't been able to find a logical explanation for it. Actually, it should be the other way around, because this mural is bigger and more likely to be damaged by natural forces."

During that explanation, Miss Level looks around and comes to the same conclusion as Petulia. She wants to talk about this with her friend, but their host seems mesmerised by the tree mural. It doesn't look like she will move away from it while they are down here. So instead Miss Level and Petulia leave their spot and walk around the room.

"Is that you?" Miss Level asks.

"Not you too."

"Tobias?" Miss Level gazes around and spots him standing next to the mural of Melchior and his followers.

"Of course." Petulia watches the young man as well. It doesn't look like he can hear them, but you never know.

"So what do you think about the tree mural?"

"Well, if the others have cracked because their predictions came true, we might try cracking the tree mural. It might destroy him." Petulia pauses. "He *is* still in that tree, isn't he?"

"He should be."

Just at that moment, a tiny fissure appears in the top left corner of the tree mural. "Oh, no!" Elizabella exclaims.

Tobias, Miss Level and Petulia rush towards her.

Elizabella points to the new fissure. "I suppose it was only a matter of time."

The others' eyes widen. This is not good. Was there any way to prevent it? Why is it only a small crack? Does that mean there is still time to stop it? Is it a countdown of sorts?

On a whim, Miss Level closes her eyes, mutters a few words, and steps forward to place her hand on the mural.

"Please don't," Elizabella starts. "You might make it worse." Then she notices the faint purple glow coming from Miss Level's outstretched palm. In awe, she stops and watches to see what will happen next.

As soon as Miss Level's hand nears the mural, a few sparks pass between the two. When she makes contact with it, her head snaps back and her eyes open wide. Panicked, Petulia grabs her friend and tries to pull her away, but can't. It is almost as if Miss Level is glued to the mural. Slowly, her head lowers to its normal position and she gently removes her hand. When she opens her eyes, the others see a faint spark of purple fading from her irises.

Petulia grabs her friend by the shoulders. "What happened? What did you see?"

As if a calm has come over her, Miss Level smiles serenely at them all. "He is still in there, but we must hurry." She looks at Petulia. "No, we can't do anything through the mural. It is only a mirror of current events until those events have passed. Then it cracks and a new mural is begun."

Immediately, Tobias starts looking around for another uncracked mural.

"You won't find an unscathed mural, Tobias. When this one was finished, he did everything in his power to keep it from coming true. So he never made another mural. What happens now has not yet been predicted, and therefore it is still open to change." Miss Level puts her hand against the mural again. Nothing happens. "His first mistake was to capture his predictions in murals. That makes them concrete and unchangeable."

Curious, Tobias asks, "What was his second mistake?"

With a mischievous smile, Miss Level turns to him. "Leaving his house unprotected."

Elizabella has by now figured out that her guests aren't normal people. Everything she just witnessed has shifted the focus of her obsession from Melchior to Miss Level. That is the only reason why she lets Miss Level do all the things she is about to do next. If Adelbert had been down here with them, he would have put a stop to it immediately.

Fortunately for Miss Level and her companions, he is still up at the top of the ladder, trying to get information out of the Head Master. It isn't going so well. His questioning only makes Dirk very nervous, and regularly leads to the two of them saying things in unison. After some time, Adelbert finds this so confusing that he leaves the tent to get some fresh air and clear his head, taking Dirk with him because he really doesn't trust him. This is a very good thing because of what happens next.

In the atrium, Miss Level asks the others to hide in a corner and huddle close together. They do so. After that, she walks into the dried-up pool, which is right in the middle of the room and, coincidentally, the entire house. She stretches out her hands to the sides, palms raised, lifts her head, and starts to mutter indiscernible words. Her palms glow purple. A rumble seems to come from deep within the earth. With a great big whoosh, all the sand in the entire house lifts up out of the open roof above the middle of the atrium. Miss Level seems to disappear in the vortex. The tent above them encounters so much pressure that it blows away, never to be seen again. The two men outside drop face down into the sand but remain unscathed. When the vortex dissipates, every nook and cranny is completely cleared of sand. Cautiously, Petulia, Tobias and Elizabella come out of hiding. Elizabella is astounded, unable to close her mouth, and even more in awe of Miss Level.

"How and why did you do that?" Petulia stands up straight, hands on her hips.

"He had some power stored in the mural." Miss Level smiles. "It is gone now. Apparently I am a good vessel for it, but I don't want to bring his own power to him when we finally face him. So, I squandered lots of it on some cleaning." Her smile becomes even brighter. "Plus, the mural showed me that his grimoire is here. We can use it against him, see where he derives his power from."

Petulia is impressed. She is usually the one with a plan, but honestly, she would never have been able to come up with something like that.

From up above, they suddenly hear Adelbert's concerned voice calling out, "Are you all right, love?"

Elizabella snaps out of her state of wonder and replies, "Perfectly fine, darling! Perfectly fine."

"What the bloody hell happened?" Adelbert's tone starts to shift from concerned to furious.

Elizabella just smiles. "Just some spring cleaning, darling."

"I am coming down there."

"No!" she shouts. "That isn't necessary. We are just going to look around for a minute and come up in about," she looks hesitantly at Miss Level, who raises ten fingers, then another five, "fifteen minutes."

"All right, love, but if you're not up here in fifteen minutes, I am coming down!"

Elizabella looks at her companions. "Well, that was quite a warning. I don't think I have ever heard him so furious before." She claps her hands in joy. "I am quite thrilled!"

Miss Level just shrugs and walks into one of the adjacent rooms. Petulia, Tobias and Elizabella follow her. They enter what looks like a bedroom. The remnants of a bed stand in the corner. Hundreds of years' worth of sand building up on it has reduced it to a pile of broken wood. However, at the other side of the room is a closet that appears to be in mint condition. Clearly a spell has been placed upon it to protect it from, well, anything, really. Miss Level squints at the closet. With narrowed eyes, she can see Melchior's signature in the spell. The other three are very curious so they try squinting as well, hoping to see what Miss Level is seeing. Petulia and Elizabella can't, but Tobias can.

"What are those squiggly lines surrounding the closet?" he asks, which makes the other two squint even harder.

Miss Level is surprised. "You can see them?"

"Yes, what are they?"

"They are power lines. The spell is like a net hanging over the closet, protecting it from any outside influence." Then she wonders, "Can you see anything else?"

He stares at the closet. Just as he is about to say no, he notices an anomaly in the squiggles around the door handle. "Yes. What is that?"

"It's his signature. It is also the way to unlock the net. Do you want to try?"

Tobias stares at her. "Are you serious?"

"Of course. I think the reason you can see the spell is because you have used his power," Miss Level explains. In response to Tobias's quizzical expression, she elaborates, "The stick. You have been using his stick."

Understanding creeps over Tobias's face.

"I am fairly certain that there is another security element to the spell. But I think you can bypass it."

"How?" Tobias frowns at her.

"Well, you are infused with his power and you are male. That might be enough to trick the spell, so to speak."

"All right, I understand." He swallows down nervous laughter. "So, what do I have to do?"

"You have to fiddle with his signature." Miss Level points at the door handle. "Squint your eyes again. When you see the signature, reach out and try to loop the left leg of the 'M' behind the right leg." She turns back to Tobias. "Do you understand what I mean?"

"Yes, I do. Anything special I need to know?"

"Not really. Just try to think like Melchior."

"*Think* like him? How am I supposed to do that?"

Miss Level shakes her head. "I didn't mean it like that. Just repeat in your head, over and over, I am Melchior. That ought to do it."

"All right." Tobias squints his eyes and reaches out slowly.

Petulia and Elizabella, who have heard the entire conversation but aren't completely sure what is going on, are looking at the other two in expectation. When they see Tobias's hand move slowly towards the door handle, they suck in a deep breath and hold it until it is all over. Tobias hears the sharp intake of breath. He pauses right in front of Melchior's signature and takes a deep breath himself. Then he slips his index and ring fingers between the squiggles of power and pulls. For Petulia and Elizabella, it is a rather funny sight to see him appear to pull at nothing.

Miss Level is also holding her breath while squinting her eyes. When she sees the left leg of the 'M' give way and follow Tobias's lead, she slowly exhales. To be completely honest, she wasn't really certain that this would work, so seeing Tobias handle the signature is a tremendous relief. When he finishes folding the left leg behind the right one, a loud snap resounds. Then the power lines disappear. He squints a little harder but the squiggles around the closet are gone.

He turns to Miss Level. "It worked?"

She hugs him close. "It worked. Good job."

Petulia, who is starting to become upset at being left out, steps up to the closet and opens the door. The grimoire is lying on the middle shelf. Hesitant to take it out, she looks at Miss Level. Her friend and Tobias are squinting at the closet but still can't see any power squiggles. A thumbs up to Petulia prompts her to lift the grimoire and close the closet again. The book is heavy and light at the same time. She quickly hands it to Miss Level because it gives her a funny sort of feeling.

He has managed to widen the crack in the bark sufficiently for his hand to slip through. The temperature outside is nice, so it must be summer or spring. A breeze allows a bit of fresh air to find its way through the gap and into the tree. He inhales deeply. It might take him longer than he anticipated but he will surely be free soon.

Suddenly, a chill runs up his spine. That is a bad omen. Someone is already working against him. If only he had some of his power...

He decides to risk it and tries to draw on the power of his grimoire. Closing his eyes, he inhales deeply, steadily. Before long, he slips into a trance. That is when he sees her. Petulia! With his grimoire in her hands! How? Why? Is she working alone? He squeezes his eyes shut, trying to hang on to the vision, to see more, but it vanishes into thin air.

With renewed passion, he grabs hold of the bark and pulls with all his might.

Seventeen

No Restraining Order Necessary

Petulia has the funny feeling that she is being watched. She looks around and sees Elizabella staring at her angrily. The reason for this is that Elizabella feels that Petulia has stolen Miss Level's moment of glory. *She* cleared the rooms of sand. *She* found the wardrobe. *She* explained everything to Tobias. And *she* should have been the one to open the wardrobe and take the book, not her so-called 'friend'.

At this point I feel I should mention that the reason Elizabella and Adelbert have lost their funding for this dig relates to the many outstanding restraining orders taken out against Elizabella by several of the committee members.

Petulia, who has no idea what is going on in their host's mind, turns nonchalantly away from her.

Completely oblivious to everything but the grimoire, Miss Level lets her hands roam over it. Magnificent. A design in relief that can't be seen, only felt, spans its entire cover. It is almost like Braille. She has no idea what the drawings depict. That is something only Melchior knows. But she doesn't get the feeling that there is a protection spell or anything like that on the book. Cautiously, she opens it. It is completely blank.

"Damn it," Petulia mutters. "This is no help at all."

Elizabella comes straight to Miss Level's defence. "I am sure that Miss Level knows what to do with it."

Petulia cocks one eyebrow to her friend, who just frowns back at her. "Do you?"

"Not really." Miss Level glances sideways at their host, not sure what just happened.

Tobias has an inkling that something bad will happen if they don't get away from their hosts as soon as possible. "Why don't we go back to the surface? The sunlight might help." He smiles at Elizabella. "Not that it is not beautiful down here, but it's quite dark, wouldn't you agree?"

"Of course." Elizabella smiles back. "I should have thought of that."

All four of them walk back to the atrium and, one by one, climb the ladder, some more slowly than others.

Tobias is the first to emerge from the hole in the roof. The first thing he notices is Adelbert pointing his rifle at Dirk. Immediately, Tobias raises his hands in surrender. "What's going on?"

"I don't bloody trust you lot." Adelbert raises his rifle even higher. "And I won't let this one go until my wife comes back out here."

"She will be up really soon. I think she was next to climb the ladder."

Unfortunately, it is Petulia whose head pops up next. This results in Adelbert putting the rifle closer to Dirk.

"Damn it. We can't leave you men alone for a minute, can we?"

Tobias shows her the tightest smile he has ever made. "Please tell me Elizabella is coming up next."

"I have no idea. She might be."

All of them stare at the hole in the roof until a thick book is shoved through it and falls to the floor. Miss Level pops up next. "I hate ladders," she mutters, not having seen what is happening in front of her.

Adelbert starts to get more anxious and trigger-happy. "Where is she? Where is my wife?"

In unison, everyone else says, "She is next."

Petulia narrows her eyes at Dirk, knowing very well that his nervousness is the reason for that happening. All he can do in response is shrug. He is, ironically, sweating bullets.

A slender hand appears at the edge of the hole. When Elizabella sees what is going on, she says, "Oh, darling, that wasn't necessary."

Adelbert lowers his rifle and runs towards her. "Yes, it was, love." Dropping the gun, he takes her face in both of his hands. "What happened down there?"

Elizabella starts rattling off everything that has happened in minute detail. While the couple are distracted, the four companions sidle closer together until they are near enough to touch. Slowly, Miss Level starts to walk backwards towards the tent where they had breakfast. The others follow her, keeping their eyes on their hosts. When they reach the tent, they quickly step inside.

"Tobias," Miss Level says, "it's your turn again. Open a portal and get us out of here, will you?"

"My pleasure," he replies, and takes out his stick. Swiftly, and with the forest in mind, he starts spinning it.

The portal opens up, so our companions grab each other's hands and step through it. Miss Level goes first, with the grimoire in her free hand. Tobias comes up last and grabs the stick right before the portal closes.

It is at this exact moment that Elizabella and Adelbert storm into the tent, having only just noticed that their guests have left them. They just see Tobias grabbing the stick and the portal closing abruptly behind him. Elizabella, who knows instinctively that she will never see Miss Level again, sinks down and starts to cry loudly. She can work around a restraining order but this is something completely different. This is vanishing into thin air. Adelbert stares at the now-empty spot in the middle of the tent, not quite believing what he has just witnessed. Knowing that he won't be able to figure it out right at this moment, he kneels down beside his wife and tries to comfort her instead.

Just as he steps out of the tree, he senses that his stick is back in this world. He smiles. And is that…? Yes, it is. His grimoire! His smile grows even bigger, with just a slight hint of evil in it.

Looking around, he dusts off his clothes while trying to figure out where he is exactly. There is nothing in the vicinity that he recognises. Surely, he is still in the same spot where they confronted him, isn't he? There are trees everywhere. Where is the path he took to get here? Wasn't there a small brook as well? He listens carefully, trying to locate the soft sound of babbling. How long has he been gone?

He starts walking to the east. They can't have moved the tree, can they?

Eighteen

Learning at the Academy

It took another two days for the snow to clear.

Not being the type of person to enjoy being cooped up, Petulia immediately opened the door, stepped out, and inhaled deeply. It was still quite cold but she didn't care. Through the open cottage door she heard Miss Level come down the stairs. Bless her heart. She was a great person, allowing Petulia to stay here for a while, but she was kind of a bubblehead, Petulia thought.

Miss Level joined her outside. "Finally." She smiled and looked around. "You have to admit, everything looks really pretty covered in snow." Her eyes darted over the little fence around the cottage, the trees and bushes, and the postbox in front of the cottage, and then she turned around. "But 'Everything in its right time and place' is my motto." She walked back inside and started rummaging around in the kitchen to fix breakfast.

Petulia stayed outside for a little while longer. Miss Level was right: everything did look really pretty. A shiver crept up her spine, reminding her that she was standing outside in the cold in nothing but her nightgown. She quickly turned and walked back into the cottage, closing the door behind her.

Miss Level had already put the kettle on for tea, and placed teacups, bread, strawberry jam and chocolate spread on the kitchen table. She was peeling an apple and slicing it into bite-sized pieces. She looked up as Petulia joined her at the table. "Did you sleep well?"

"Sure." Petulia took two slices of bread and reached for the chocolate spread.

"I thought I noticed it warming up a bit last night, so I am very pleased to see that the snow has melted enough for us to leave." Miss Level popped a piece of apple in her mouth and chewed thoughtfully.

"Should we call on God to set up a time to go to Edmundtown?"

"It can wait until after breakfast," Miss Level said around her mouthful of apple.

The kettle started to whistle, so Miss Level stood up and lifted it off the stove. She returned to the table and filled the teacups.

At that moment, God's face appeared in the bowl of water. "The snow has started to melt. I can leave the house. How is everything with you?" He spoke rapidly and excitedly.

"So much for enjoying a quiet breakfast," muttered Petulia. God had interrupted their breakfast every day during their confinement, grumbling about how he still couldn't leave his house and how he felt like a prisoner.

Miss Level put the kettle back on the stove. "Maybe you should go out and see if you can find out anything about Melchior?"

"Great idea." God's face disappeared.

Petulia frowned. She had been doing that a lot lately; must have something to do with the woman in front of her. "Shouldn't we have talked about where and when to meet up?"

Miss Level waved her hand in dismissal. "Oh, he will be back in about half an hour. We can discuss everything then. But now, I want to enjoy my breakfast. Maybe I will check *The Arcane News* while I am at it." She went into the study to fetch the piece of parchment that updated every day around midnight.

Petulia sighed and smiled. Her new friend might be a little cuckoo but she did have great ideas occasionally. She picked up a teabag and dropped it gently into her cup.

Miss Level was already scanning the parchment as she walked back into the living room. "There is a lot of speculation about the cause of the snowstorm. All of it wrong, of course. Oh please, as if there really is a hole in the sky that can cause serious temperature fluctuations. Amateurs." She shook her head as she sat back down at the table.

They ate breakfast together in silence, Miss Level perusing *The Arcane News* and Petulia lost in thought about Melchior and his whereabouts.

Promptly half an hour after his first appearance that day, God's face popped up in the water bowl. "Are you still having breakfast?" he asked incredulously.

Miss Level didn't even look up from *The Arcane News*. "Yes, we are." She shoved a slice of bread and strawberry jam into her mouth and took a big bite.

"Well," – God's chest puffed up with a sense of superiority; they couldn't see this, of course, but they could hear it in his voice – "I have been out and about while you were lazing around eating breakfast."

"And did you find out anything?"

"Well, no," God conceded, his chest deflating.

Miss Level smiled. "Strange how you have found out nothing, while I have found out so many things while sitting here, eating my breakfast."

God glared at her. "Get on with it, then."

"Well, Austencia has been found. She was lying in a ditch near the north wall of Edmundtown. You know, where that guard said he saw a dark figure hovering around and howling?" Miss Level turned the parchment towards Petulia, who craned her head to see what she was pointing at. "There is a picture here that shows a heap of snow where there shouldn't have been one. When they cleared it this morning, they found Austencia's body underneath it. Apparently, she had a giant burn mark on her back." She looked at Petulia. "That is why it is in *The Arcane News*. A burn mark during a snowstorm? It is a little weird."

Petulia's face blanched. "Do you think that's how Melchior killed her?"

Miss Level shrugged. "I don't know, but it makes sense. When Austencia was casting the snow spell, she would have gone cold, almost becoming ice herself. Fire would be a sure way to kill her while she was in that state. And if it happened during the casting of the spell, it explains why the snowfall stopped. But the temperature wouldn't have started to rise and the snow wouldn't have started to melt. Not until the natural elements found a way to get through. It is kind of like everything froze."

"Poor Austencia," God murmured. "I knew her. She wasn't that bad. Just made a few bad decisions." He shook his head. "What a way to go."

"Well," Miss Level interrupted his musings, "this just proves that Melchior has really gone to the dark side. We have to stop him."

"You are right," God agreed. "Have you thought of any other people you want to join us? If this is the kind of magic Melchior does, we will need all the help we can get."

"Yes, we will. Dirk would be a good choice."

"Who is Dirk?" Petulia asked.

"He is the new headmaster of the Academy and he is really good, although a little nervous sometimes."

"All right. Fine by me," God agreed. "Anyone else?"

"Not that I can think of at the moment." Grudgingly, Miss Level asked, "Were you able to contact the Briar sisters?"

"No." God pouted. "They haven't replied to my message yet."

They probably think you're not worthy, Miss Level thought, but she held her tongue. Smiling a little, she said, "We should probably go to Edmundtown and check out the north wall. We will stop at the Academy and fill in the headmaster. Maybe he can join us at the wall and help us right away." She looked from Petulia to God's face and back. "How about we meet at the Academy in an hour?"

"Sounds good." And with those words, God's face disappeared from the water.

Petulia stared at the bowl. "Can we tip that away now? It kind of unnerves me to think that he can just pop up there at any time."

Miss Level shrugged. "We will leave it for just a little while longer. It is probably the safest way to communicate while Melchior is out there."

"All right, then," Petulia conceded.

An hour later, Petulia and Miss Level were standing in front of the Academy.

"Damn it, where is he?" Petulia was not a patient woman. She was standing with her hands on her hips, tapping her foot on the steps.

"He will be here. Just give him a few more minutes." Miss Level turned to regard the place where she had gone to school as a little girl. That was ages ago. The building had lost some of its former glory but was still quite impressive.

"Finally!" Petulia caught sight of God moving down the street towards them. "Hurry up!" she yelled.

It had no effect whatsoever on God, who still walked leisurely with his hands in his pants pockets. When he reached them, he said, "What is the point of hurrying? The headmaster isn't going anywhere. And the wall isn't going anywhere either." He moved around Petulia and walked through the door.

Miss Level just shrugged and followed. She was used to this behaviour. God always wanted to show that he was better than the rest. It would be even worse when he started talking to Dirk.

When they entered the building, the first thing they noticed was how quiet it was. The place should have been bustling with children. Where was everyone? They walked silently around the ground floor. Nobody. Not a soul.

"Is this normal?" Petulia gazed into another empty room.

"Maybe they cancelled all lessons due to the weather?" Miss Level wasn't sure, but that could be the reason.

They passed another empty classroom. "That could be it, but then why was the door open?" Petulia shivered. "It doesn't make any sense."

"Right." God was getting tired of this. "Let's just go straight up to the second floor to the headmaster's office. If Dirk isn't here, something is really wrong."

He was right, of course. Ever since Dirk had been made headmaster, he had never been more than two feet away from this building. Of course, the job came with a fully furnished apartment adjacent to the headmaster's office, so why would he ever leave?

The three of them headed back to the main hallway and up the stairs. They passed no one. The entire building was silent. On the second floor, they made at once for the headmaster's office. The door was slightly ajar. A soft, rhythmic sound came from within. As they crept closer, it became clear that the sound was a snore.

God pushed open the door firmly, causing it to hit the wall with a loud bang. The figure behind the desk woke abruptly and tried to say something. This was rather difficult given the gag in his mouth. God, Petulia and Miss Level stared at him.

Dirk was tied to his chair, wearing only his underwear. "Hmph." He pleaded with his eyes for them to release him.

Miss Level shook her head as she walked up to him. "What have you done now?" She took the gag out of his mouth.

"Nothing, I swear I haven't done anything." His voice sounded hoarse, as if he hadn't used it for a few days.

"So what happened?" Miss Level picked at the knotted rope around his wrists.

"I don't know. I was ambushed." Dirk looked at them. "I was just walking down the hallway, making sure that everything was ready for classes to begin, when I was suddenly knocked out. And when I came to, I was tied to this chair."

"Did you see who knocked you out?" Petulia asked.

"No, I didn't." Dirk shook his head sadly. "I just hope it wasn't one of our students. I have faith in every single one of them, but if they did this…" His voice trailed off.

"Speaking of students," God said, "shouldn't there be some here?"

Dirk frowned. "What do you mean?"

"I mean, we didn't see any while we were walking through the school."

"That doesn't make any sense."

Miss Level released Dirk's wrists before starting on the knot around his chest. "Did you tell them to stay home because of the weather?"

"What weather?" He stared at her in confusion.

"You didn't see the snow?"

"Snow? What snow? Summer just started. There is no snow."

The three others glanced at each other.

"So you were tied up before the snow fell?" Miss Level asked.

"Well, I don't know. I was in this room with my back to the window."

"All right," Miss Level said. "Once you are free, we are going to check the entire Academy to see if anything is missing."

"Missing?" Dirk's face paled. The moment he was free, he jumped out of his chair and raced through the door.

After the first moment of surprise, Miss Level, Petulia and God followed him. They could just see him round the corner.

"What the hell is he doing?" God cursed, trying to run as fast as he could, which wasn't very fast at all.

"Don't know," Petulia answered, picking up her skirt so that she could pick up her pace.

When they reached the corner, Dirk was standing stock-still outside one of the classrooms. "He is gone. Alan is gone."

As the others joined him, Miss Level asked, "Who is Alan?"

"He is...uhm..." Dirk thought a little before turning to them. "He is a centaur."

"What?!" they yelled in unison.

"Listen, it is not what you think." Dirk held up his hands. "Alan came to me last year. He was sick and tired of the reputation centaurs have."

"Oh, you mean the raping and pillaging?" God asked incredulously.

"Exactly." Dirk opened the door to the classroom and walked in. It was in chaos: chairs toppled over, books everywhere, the teacher's desk upended. "He explained to me that centaurs aren't

156

like that. They can be rather violent, but that makes them good warriors. And they do have a lot of sex, but they don't go around raping other beings. That reputation started after a miller's daughter fell in love with a centaur and they were found...you know...in the woods. The miller couldn't accept it and made himself and everyone else believe it was rape."

"And you believe this story?" Petulia quirked one eyebrow.

"Yes, I do." Dirk glanced around the trashed room. "And Alan has been a wonderful teacher. There have been a few problems with an unusual sexual appetite among his students, but apparently centaurs can have that effect on people. Nothing ever came of it. And parents were told in advance that one of the teachers was a centaur so that they could decide if they wanted their kids to take his class or not."

Looking around the classroom, Miss Level remarked, "It doesn't look like he went willingly."

"No, he didn't," Dirk replied. "He really liked it here. Said it a thousand times. He was so happy that he was able to help change the image of centaurs by teaching here. Smart man, too. He wouldn't have just gone quietly with anyone." A tear slid slowly down his cheek. "I hope he is all right. Who would do this?"

Miss Level glanced at Petulia. Could Melchior have done this? But why? What could he possibly want with a centaur? Of course, if he had taken Alan, it would make sense for him to make sure that there were no students around to stop him. And if they really liked Alan, as the headmaster implied, they would have tried to, and Melchior would have been outnumbered.

"So did Melchior make the snowstorm happen just so that he could abduct a centaur?" God snorted. "That doesn't make any sense to me."

"Of course it doesn't." Miss Level rolled her eyes at him. "It does to me, though. He wouldn't have wanted to have students interfering, and what better way to stop them than to block them from being here with – oh, I don't know – an impassable snowstorm?" She turned to Dirk. "Unfortunately, Dirk *was* here, so Melchior had to make sure he didn't interfere either. Knocking him out and tying him up worked brilliantly."

Dirk kept gazing from one to the other. "Melchior? What does he have to do with anything?"

"Right, he doesn't know yet." Petulia took a step closer to him. "How well do you know Melchior?"

Dirk plopped down into his chair. "Melchior did what?"

After he'd put on some clothes, Miss Level had filled him in, but he still didn't seem to grasp the idea of Melchior being evil just yet. It might take him a little while longer. All of a sudden, he blinked and vanished, leaving Petulia, Miss Level and God standing, confused, in his office.

But he didn't care. He had gone to his safe place. The place where he could let go of some of his frustration. It was near the sea, on top of a cliff, where the rumble of waves crashing into the cliff side was almost deafening. He took a deep breath, opened his mouth, and yelled as loud as he could. At first it was only a meaningless scream of frustration, but it soon evolved into words. "How? Why? Are you kidding me?" He screamed at the top of his lungs, knowing that nobody would hear these words. "I just spent three days tied to a chair because of you? I thought you were my friend. How could you do this to me?" He raised his arms in frustration. "I should never have told you about the centaur." He turned around, breathing heavily.

After a few deep breaths, he turned back to the sea. "Aaaargh! I should have trusted my instincts. I knew I saw a glint in your eyes when I first mentioned him. I should have stopped talking, stopped confiding in you, but I convinced myself it wasn't real, that I was just seeing things." He turned back around, stomping away from the edge of the cliff. His throat was beginning to hurt, so he started mumbling to himself instead, crossing his arms in front of him. "Should have kicked you out right there and then. And what are you going to do with him anyway? He is not like the others, the ones you hear all those stories about. You should have realised that the moment I told you he was going to teach at the Academy." Suddenly, his head whipped up. "Or is that exactly why you have taken him? He can't give you anything, you know." His hand rubbed his face. "Where are you? And what are you doing now?"

He pinched his nose, opened his eyes, and blinked again. His sudden reappearance in his office startled Miss Level, Petulia and God. They had been looking for him. In fact, Petulia was still on her hands and knees, looking under the desk, when his legs reappeared next to her. She hit her head on the underside of the desktop before she rose from that position. Miss Level was standing near the door, which she had only just closed. She had been looking in the hallway for him.

God had the open doors of the headmaster's closet in his hands. He had been examining it, having told the ladies that he just wanted to check if Dirk wasn't in there, but to be honest he just wanted to see which supplies the headmaster had. Caught red-handed, he blushed and, before turning around, said, "Well, he is not in here." Not very convincing. Then he turned to the desk. "Oh, there you are. Look, ladies, he is back."

But Dirk didn't notice any of this. "All right, I believe you are telling the truth about Melchior."

Petulia squinted her eyes at him. "Why do you say that? What made you change your mind?"

He sagged down into his desk chair and sighed deeply. "I believe it because he stole Alan from me. I saw something in his eyes when I told him about Alan but I dismissed it immediately. Should have trusted my instincts."

"But what could he possibly do with a centaur?" Petulia asked.

God snorted again. "Maybe he wants to start an orgy."

Petulia took two quick steps towards him and slapped him on the back of the head.

"Ouch!" God rubbed his head and scowled at her.

"You are such an idiot." Petulia rested her hands on her hips in her usual pose. "Not all men think like that."

"It was just a thought."

"Well, keep those thoughts to your damn self." She turned away from him and moved closer to the desk. "Headmaster, what do you think?"

"I don't know." Dirk scratched his head. "The only thing I can think of is that he wants to use Alan as an army strategist, but that doesn't make sense. Melchior doesn't have an army and Alan would never participate willingly in something like that."

Miss Level had been unusually quiet during this conversation. "But what if he forces him? Would he do it then?"

Dirk reflected on this. "Melchior would have to have some major leverage. Alan is a peaceful centaur. He really is. I just don't see him suddenly becoming violent."

"What if he uses a spell?" Miss Level whispered.

God's head snapped towards her. "What did you just say?"

Miss Level lifted her head and pronounced deliberately, "What if he uses a spell?"

"How do you know about that?" God cleared the space between them so quickly that Miss Level startled and stepped back. "Who told you?"

Miss Level swallowed. "Nobody told me anything. I was just thinking that there are spells for all occasions. Why wouldn't there be one for something like this?"

"Like what?" Petulia asked curiously.

Miss Level glanced at her; anything to look away from God's piercing gaze. "Like forcing your will onto someone."

Petulia whistled. "That would be a great spell. I know a certain boy I would like to force never to eat from your house ever again."

With a roll of her eyes, Miss Level replied, "Of course you would. But just think about it. What if you could use a spell to take away someone's free will, their capacity to make decisions for themselves? To create someone who will always follow you wherever you go, and who will always do whatever you want them to?" For a moment, she seemed lost in thought, looking at the ground. "That would be just awful."

Dirk had been eyeing God ever since he'd suddenly walked up to Miss Level in a peculiar fashion. He poked him with a pen. "What were you going on about?"

"Who? Me?" Feigning ignorance, God quickly turned away from all of them. "Nothing. I don't know what you are talking about."

"Yes, you do." Dirk got up from his chair. "You know exactly what it would take, don't you? You know which spell Melchior could use." He stabbed his short little index finger into God's chest. "Admit it."

With a great sigh, God finally relented. "Fine. I might know of a spell he could use."

Immediately, Miss Level turned to him. "And does Melchior know this?"

Hesitantly, God nodded.

"Well, that is just great." Petulia threw up her arms. "When were you going to tell us about that little gem?"

"I didn't... I wasn't..." God sputtered. "It's not like that. One night, we were discussing hypothetical things and this one came up."

Petulia glared at him. "What do you mean, 'This one came up'?"

God sighed. "It was all hypothetical. Or so I thought. I never once imagined that Melchior was serious about that." He glanced around at the others. "You know – wanting people to follow him, to take his word for truth. To mindlessly do whatever they were commanded." He dropped his gaze, ashamed.

"But you have reconsidered this now?" Cautiously, Miss Level stepped a little closer to him. "You think he might actually use this spell?"

Feeling like he had a friend in Miss Level, God looked only at her, trying very hard to ignore the angry glares of the other two. "Yes, I think he just might."

"Is there any way to counteract the spell?"

"No, but you can get out of it, if you are strong enough." He sighed. "Unfortunately, it takes years of training."

"How?" Miss Level crossed her arms, waiting patiently, yet highly curious, for the answer.

"Well," God took a deep breath before continuing, "it has the same mechanism as a freeze spell, but it's a lot stronger. A freeze spell immobilises the person immediately. However, if their will is strong enough, they can unfreeze bit by bit until they're completely free." A shy smile spread over his face. "I have been able to do that a few times now. It comes in handy when you have a few exes who like freezing you."

"And how do you go about unfreezing?" Dirk asked, intrigued.

"It sounds silly but you just have to want to not be frozen any more."

"Right." Dirk sat back down in his chair. "If that is all." All hope left his mind. He knew perfectly well that of all the people in this room, his will was the weakest. He was done for.

Miss Level, however, was still intrigued. She made a note to start practising this will thing as soon as she could. You never knew when it might come in handy. She was fairly certain that it would work against other spells as well.

"Just one question." Petulia interrupted everyone's musing. "Why didn't he use the spell on Alan?" When the only replies she got were blank stares from her companions, she elaborated. "You saw the classroom, didn't you? He clearly didn't go without a fight. So why didn't Melchior use that spell?"

God thought for a while. What was he missing? Ah, no – the question was: what was *Melchior* missing? "He would have needed a personal possession of the subject. Only then will the spell work."

Dirk, who had been rather quiet until then, stood up. "Hang on." He left the room, leaving the others perplexed. When he re-entered the office, his expression was grave. "Alan had one item that meant the world to him. It was a rock, of all things. It was part of the hill his clan lived on." He swallowed hard. "The rock is no longer in his classroom."

"Well, that explains why no other part of the school was trashed." Miss Level moved over to him and hugged him. "I am sorry, Dirk, but I think Alan put up quite a fight until Melchior cast his spell."

"I know." The headmaster cleared his throat loudly, then gently pushed away from Miss Level. "We need to do something. We need to find a way to protect everyone."

Miss Level smiled. "You're right. And I know just where to start." She faced the three of them. "We should examine Austencia's body."

Three horrified faces stared back at her.

"We need to know how exactly she died, so that we can prepare ourselves." She grabbed her bag and went to leave. Sensing that no one was following her, she turned back. "Come on, then!"

Not quite sure what else they could do, Dirk shrugged and followed her. God was slightly more reluctant, annoyed that he wasn't the one who'd come up with the idea. By now Petulia had figured out that Miss Level's ideas, although occasionally somewhat weird, always paid out, and so she took a last look around the room before catching up with the others in the hallway.

Nineteen

An Astonishing Revelation

It must have been quite the sight: two witches and two wizards sitting on a bench in Town Hall, waiting patiently for Master Reedy, the general practitioner of Edmundtown. He was a good man but had no knowledge whatsoever of the arcane. To be completely honest, he was rather blind to it. To him, the four people waiting there were just ordinary people. Nothing weird about them. To many others, the same four people were clearly 'off' and were usually given a wide berth when passing them on the street.

"Ah, yes," Master Reedy exclaimed enthusiastically, "you had some questions about the woman in the snow?"

Miss Level rose from her seat and took the lead in the conversation. She was fairly certain that the others still had no idea what they were doing there. "Yes, we do." She shook the man's hand. "We are students of…uhm… General Practitioner Uleigh in…uhm… Heaven."

"Really?" Master Reedy frowned. "I must say, I have never heard of the man."

"That doesn't surprise me." Miss Level smiled at him. "But he has certainly heard of you. He speaks very highly of you." She patted him on the arm. "Especially about the way you have handled the woman in the snow. That's why he sent us here: to admire your work and see what we can learn from you." Gesturing behind her back to urge the others to stand as well, she smiled sadly at Master Reedy. "Unfortunately, Master Uleigh could not join us. He has taken ill himself."

"How unfortunate indeed. I would have loved to have met the man in person." Master Reedy was already imagining the conversations he could have with an esteemed colleague. There weren't a lot of general practitioners around, and since his own mentor had died five years ago he had missed being able to 'talk shop'. Suddenly realising that he had drifted off into his own thoughts, he blinked and turned back to Miss Level. "Of course, I would be happy to help tutor you in this case. Follow me."

They entered a small, chilled room. In the middle was a stone table on which the body of Austencia was laid out. Master Reedy stepped over to her right side, gesturing to the others to take up positions to her left. The four companions silently complied.

"So, this is the woman that was found at the edge of the forest. She was covered by a big pile of snow, so she must have died during the snowstorm."

God leaned in and whispered in Miss Level's ear, "Or been buried by it afterwards."

"Most likely," she replied out of the corner of her mouth.

Master Reedy was so caught up in his explanations that he didn't notice any of this. "What is most peculiar is the burn mark on her back." He reached over and tipped the body so that her back was exposed to the four onlookers.

The rest of what he said never registered with any of them. They were staring at a giant wound that was clearly a magical burn. The ragged edge made such an outline that it looked like a signature. Miss Level leaned in closer. Yes, that was definitely a signature. It had Melchior written all over it. Before she realised what she was doing, she extended her hand to touch the mark. A sharp intake of breath came from two mouths, but it was already too late: her fingers touched the body. Strangely, nothing happened. She straightened up.

"Well, thank you, Master Reedy." Not caring that she had just interrupted him, she continued, "But I am afraid we must be going now." And with those words, she spun on her heels and quickly exited the room. The others followed her lead.

It was only after the four strange persons had left that Master Reedy realised that it was quite uncommon for one mentor to have four apprentices at the same time. Wasn't there a rule about how many apprentices one master could have?

"What happened?" The minute they exited Town Hall, God grabbed Miss Level's arm.

"Nothing," she replied. "Nothing happened."

"How could that be?" Dirk joined in. "I was sure that sparks would fly once you touched her."

"I know." Miss Level shook her head. "I don't know what happened. I hadn't planned on touching her but there was something about that mark."

The sound of a foot tapping on the floor caused them to look at Petulia. "Can someone please explain why there would have been sparks?" Standing with her hands on her hips, she raised one eyebrow in question.

"How can you call yourself a witch if you don't even know the most basic things?" God roared at her.

"Shush." Quickly, Miss Level scanned the street to see if anyone had heard the outburst. "Let's go back to the Academy and think about this."

"Right you are, Miss Level," Dirk replied, and led the way.

Sulkily, Petulia and God followed.

They reached the Academy and decided to visit the canteen, as they were all getting hungry. Usually around this time, the canteen would be filled with students and their accompanying noise. But the headmaster had not yet sent out a message to say that they were welcome to come back, so the four companions attempted to relieve the school of the food that would otherwise go to waste. Sitting at one of the long tables with a nice spread between them, they delved into it.

After a few distracted bites, Miss Level mumbled, "I don't understand."

Straight away, Petulia exclaimed, "Finally, I am going to get an answer to my question."

"Oh, right, I forgot." Miss Level smiled apologetically. "When a witch or wizard dies, their power stays in their body as a sort of residual energy. If another witch or wizard touches the body, that contact will manifest that energy in the form of sparks."

Petulia frowned. "But that didn't happen."

"Exactly." Miss Level stared at the sandwich in her hand. "But *why* didn't it happen?"

A heavy silence fell over the table, during which everyone pondered that question.

After a few minutes, Petulia broke the silence. "And this *always* happens?"

"Yes," the others replied in unison.

"Are you sure?"

"Yes." Again in unison, but this time eliciting glares from Miss Level and God towards Dirk.

Petulia didn't notice. "And it's a witch's power that turns into this energy thing?"

"Yes." More glares towards Dirk, who just shrugged.

"And it's the witch's power's energy thing that makes the sparks?"

"Yes."

Dirk took a few spoons full of soup, thinking that it might not happen again if he couldn't talk himself.

"So no sparks, no energy. And no energy, no power?" Petulia scratched her head. "That doesn't seem right."

But Dirk's head shot up. "Hang on. I think you are on to something." He dropped his spoon, which clattered to the floor, and sprinted out of the canteen.

"I am getting used to seeing him run away," God mused.

"It's better than the unison thing," Miss Level replied. "That one is quite annoying."

Petulia gazed from one to the other. "What unison thing?"

But before a reply could come, Dirk rushed back into the canteen. "Found it!" Slightly out of breath, he sat back down, dropping a thick volume onto the table. As Miss Level tried to read the cover, he started leafing through it.

"Ah, *The Encyclopaedia Magicae*." Miss Level nodded wisely.

Dirk's left index finger rose into the air. "Here it is." Following the words with his right index finger, he read aloud, "'Although unknown to most practitioners of magic, there are several spells that can drain the power of a witch or wizard, be it knowingly or unknowingly.'"

"What do they mean, unknowingly?" Petulia frowned at him.

He flapped his hand at her. "Hang on, hang on." Scanning the rest of the page, he mumbled some of the words he was reading.

The other three turned away from him slightly and went back to finishing their meal.

Not too long after that, the left index finger rose again. "Listen to this. 'It is possible to inadvertently drain your own power when you try out a spell that is too big for you.'"

"What?" Petulia interrupted. "How can a spell be too big?"

Dirk looked at her. "Well, not every witch has the same amount of power. There are forest witches and sea witches who spend their days listening to nature and stepping in where needed. But they don't have that much power, just what is necessary to heal animals or mend trees. So if they were to, I don't know, try a shapeshifting spell, that would most likely drain them. Not deliberately, of course." A small chuckle escaped him.

"Of course," Petulia replied sarcastically. Then, before Dirk could get back to his reading, she continued, "And if that happens, can they get it back?"

"If the power has not been drained completely, it will restore itself gradually over time, but it will probably never get back to the same level as before. Fortunately, most practitioners sense immediately when something is going wrong with a spell and will abruptly stop whatever they are doing." He glanced back at the book.

God, who had been listening as well, hazarded, "I am sensing a 'but' here."

"Yes, you are quite right. A big 'but' as well." Dirk looked up, not registering the sniggers from his companions. "If power is *deliberately* drained, it will not return at all. In some cases it might even cause the affected person to die."

Miss Level paled. "Is that what happened to Austencia?"

"Not quite." Dirk swallowed hard. "I believe she was hit with two separate spells: one to drain her of her powers, and one to kill her with immense pain."

The others dropped their food-filled hands to the table, suddenly not hungry any more. "Right."

Twenty

Secrets of the Grimoire

Tobias and the others rematerialise not too far from where Petulia and Miss Level live. They all agree that they are a bit hungry, so they decide to have something to eat at the witches' house. Miss Level is thrilled, of course. She has missed Gabriel, and hopes he isn't mad because she has been gone for so long.

When they reach the cottage, Petulia enters first and is greeted by the smells of freshly baked goodies. Any other day, this would have upset her to no end, but today she is just too hungry. Before she realises it, she says, "Hello, Gabriel. Thank you for preparing food." Then she lets the others in. "We have some guests."

Gabriel is happy that they are back. He waves politely at the two strange men who walk through the door. But when Miss Level walks in, he immediately slings the towel he was using for the washing-up over the back of a chair and rushes towards her. He lifts her up and kisses her right there and then, not caring that the others are watching. Miss Level, for her part, loves the effect she has on Gabriel. She wraps her arms around his neck and kisses him right back. Tobias and Dirk are actually astonished to find a man in the witches' house, let alone to witness such a happy encounter between one of the witches and said man. When Gabriel sets Miss Level back down, he turns around shyly and goes back to the washing-up.

Petulia, who has witnessed everything as well, finds herself not reacting as she usually would to this great display of affection. She actually finds it endearing. "Come on, let's sit down and eat something." She goes over to the cupboard. "You too, Gabriel. I will finish the washing-up after we have eaten."

Astonished, Gabriel does as he is told. He likes this side of Petulia; not the grumpy side he's become used to seeing lately. She takes some plates and sets them out on the table. Everyone grabs one and sets to it. Cakes, crumpets, bread, pudding and so on – the table is strewn with them. Gabriel shrugs shyly. He loves to bake, but it has also been something to keep his mind from worrying about Miss Level. He knows that she will tell him all about the strange men and what has happened. But that doesn't mean he didn't worry while she was gone.

Miss Level knows her man, so she leans in closer to him and whispers, "The young man is called Tobias. He's the one who was spilling magic. We found him rather quickly, but stumbled upon another problem. See, he used a stick for his magic, but it is a special stick. It came from a tree in which we entrapped an evil wizard years ago. We fear the wizard might have escaped, so we went to the Witches' Guild, where the Head Master – that's the old man – said he would help us. We went to the evil wizard's home and found his grimoire, and then we came back here." She kisses Gabriel's cheek. "That's the short version."

He smiles at her, feeling quite content in this moment.

Tobias has never before seen so many baked goods in a single place that isn't a bakery. The smell is mouth-watering. He grabs a lemon tart and bites into it. "Mmm. This is the best I have ever eaten." He quickly grabs another before there are none left.

Dirk pops the last bite of a scone into his mouth. "Heavenly." Then he takes his knife and cuts a piece of chocolate cake.

Before this, Petulia always ignored what Gabriel baked. Now she has to admit that he really does have a talent. Maybe she shouldn't be so hard on him. And if he lets her do the dishes, she will be fine with him cooking. Around a mouthful of blueberry cupcake, she mumbles, "We need a plan."

The others just nod, unable to speak with delicious goodies in their mouths.

"Maybe we should consult *The Big Book of Dale* first. See if we can get Melchior's grimoire to divulge his secrets."

Another nod from her companions, although Tobias has no idea what *The Big Book of Dale* is.

Petulia takes a deep breath. "After that, I think we should go to the tree."

Three gulps resound, and then a flurry of words all jumbled together.

"Isn't that dangerous?" is Tobias's first reaction.

"Let's see what the book says first," Miss Level replies.

"Brilliant idea, but we have to prepare ourselves," Dirk says.

Petulia is most surprised by his reaction. The others she expected, but his? Did he just agree with her? As she watches their facial expressions she can only conclude that her first impression was correct: he did in fact agree with her. Gripped by confusion, she stands up and walks into the study. She takes *The Big Book of Dale* off the bookshelf and returns to the kitchen. The book thumps onto the table, startling the rest of them, who have continued eating. "It is your turn now," she says to Miss Level, who stands up and approaches the book.

Tobias and Dirk frown at Petulia. "Why don't you look through the book?" they say (in unison – what else?).

"Let's just say that the book likes her better than me." Petulia sits back down. After checking out the goodies that are left over – the others have really gone to town on them – she selects an apple and cinnamon cupcake and bites into it.

Miss Level waves her hands above the closed book. She mutters, "Grimoire" and "Melchior" over and over until the pages start to flutter and it opens up to a specific page. She swiftly peruses it and frowns. "How will this help us?"

Dirk, who has always been interested in *The Big Book of Dale*, joins her eagerly. He has heard so many great things about this book. Being in the vicinity of it really makes his day. It is supposed to have all the answers. But for the life of him, he can't understand why it has opened up to this page. Petulia, Tobias and Gabriel become curious as well. Simultaneously, they rise from the table and join the other two.

"A locator spell?" Petulia asks. "Why would it send us a locator spell? The grimoire is right here. We just need to see what is written in it."

"Of course!" Miss Level exclaims. "We need to find the words." She slaps herself on the forehead.

"Of course," Petulia echoes, slightly sarcastically. "We might as well give it a try." She points to a small cupboard at the other side of the room. "Dirk, would you grab some candles from that cupboard?"

To her utter surprise, he complies without any argument. To be quite honest, he is just as confused as she is. Why is he taking orders from her? And why isn't his eye twitching after hearing her say his name? He opens the cupboard and finds five candlesticks and a box of matches waiting for him. At the same time, Petulia asks Tobias and Gabriel to clear the table, which they do promptly. Miss Level is already looking for the right herbs. They will need sage, thyme, parsley, coriander, and drake root. She ties the dried herbs together with a small piece of string. Petulia herself grabs a cloth from the sink and starts to clean the table. A pentagram is marked out with more of the string that was used to bind the herbs. At each point of it, a candlestick is placed. In the middle, Miss Level puts the grimoire. Each of the persons assembled is positioned at a tip of the pentagram and right in front of a candle. Dirk takes a match and lights the candles.

When everything is ready, Miss Level puts the bundle of herbs to the flame of one of the candles, whereupon it starts to smoke. She begins to mutter again, this time in Latin. While chanting the words of the spell, she follows the lines of the pentagram with the smoking bundle of herbs and ends the trail above the grimoire. The moment she stops chanting, she drops the smoking herbs. They fall apart in ashes before reaching the grimoire. When they land on the cover, the ashes seep into the book. Everyone stares at the grimoire, half-expecting it to start burning. When nothing else happens, Miss Level blows out the candle before her. The others follow her lead and blow out theirs. The smoke from the candles circles back to the grimoire and creeps between the pages.

Fairly certain that everything has been done correctly, Miss Level opens the grimoire. Beautiful penmanship greets her. "So," – she turns to the others – "how are we going to find what we need to destroy or recapture Melchior?"

Tobias frowns at her. "Can't you do the same thing you just did with the other book?"

"I'm afraid it's not that simple." Miss Level smiles ruefully. "This is not my book. And I am pretty sure that it doesn't like us very much. Otherwise, it would not have hidden its words in the first place. So, it would be very surprising if it listened to any spell I conjure up."

"So what do we do now?"

"Is anyone really good at speed-reading?"

Hesitantly, Dirk raises his hand. "I am actually trained in speed-reading."

"All right, then. It is settled. You will go through the grimoire while we teach Tobias a few fundamental basics of magic. Just in case."

Petulia interrupts, "Actually, I think *you* should teach Tobias. You are better at it than I am, anyway. I will help Dirk." At the astonished looks on her companions' faces, she sticks out her chin in a very stubborn Petulia way. "Two pairs of eyes are better than one. Right?"

"Sure," everyone replies in unison.

Immediately, Petulia turns to Dirk. "Unless you don't want me to, of course?"

"Uhm, no, that's fine." He gulps. "Two pairs of eyes are indeed better." A crimson colour creeps up his neck to his cheeks. He takes the grimoire from the table and turns quickly to the sofa in the middle of the living room. Petulia follows him.

Miss Level is vexed. She has no idea what has come over her friend. Petulia hates Dirk. She avoids going to the Guild headquarters just to make sure she won't see him. That's how much she detests the man. And now she is voluntarily sitting next to him, reading from the same book. A vague sense of recognition swims through Miss Level. She glances at Gabriel, who is looking at her with love in his eyes. Then she glances back at her friend and Dirk and thinks she might just have seen a glimpse of the same in their eyes. She smiles: they probably don't even know it themselves. Gabriel wiggles his eyebrows at her, clearly thinking exactly the same thing.

Miss Level rolls her eyes in response, grabs Tobias by the arm, and pulls him towards the door. Over her shoulder, she announces to the others, "We are going outside to practise."

Vague sounds of acknowledgement come from the sofa.

He has been walking for over an hour and still hasn't made it out of the forest. He really can't remember it being so dense before. The sun isn't able to reach the ground at all, which makes him stumble a lot. He is growing more furious by the minute. Of course, it doesn't help that he has yet to find anything magical in this place. The only good thing is that he still senses his grimoire close by.

He hopes like hell that he isn't walking in the wrong direction. Vain as he is, he is quite certain that his internal compass will only lead him the right way. But what is taking so long?

He can't understand how anybody can enjoy walking just for the hell of it. Those people are mad. Completely, utterly mad. If he had his way, walking would be banned from now on. Only teleportation or motorised vehicles would be allowed. How he misses teleportation! Just think of a specific place and there you are. Brilliant!

He trips over a tree root that sticks up from the ground. Enraged, he turns and kicks the root several times as hard as he can. The end result is a very painful foot which causes him to limp even more.

Gabriel is cleaning the kitchen when he suddenly hears "Eureka!" from the sofa. He actually forgot that Petulia and Dirk were sitting there. They have been so quiet.

"What?" Petulia asks. "What did you find?"

"Well, I am not quite sure if it would work on him, but look at this." Dirk points to a place halfway down the page he has been speed-reading.

Petulia bends over the book and reads the paragraph he is pointing to. "It certainly looks promising. Wait – there is a reference to another page. Turn to page fifty-eight, will you?"

Dirk does as requested. Silently, they read the page. The further they get, the wider their smiles become.

"That, my dear Dirk, is very promising indeed."

On a whim, Petulia kisses his cheek, which startles him so much he nearly drops the book altogether. Fumbling to keep it on his lap and open at the right page, he stares at her. Petulia, who isn't really sure why she did that, waits for some kind of response, but nothing comes.

"Well," – she gets up from the sofa – "I will just get the others so they can see it as well." And with those words, she goes outside.

Dirk is vexed. What just happened? And more importantly, why did he like it?

He is still trying to wrap his head around it when the others come back inside. They assemble around the sofa and quickly read what he and Petulia have found.

"That might actually work." Miss Level sounds surprised, which she is. She didn't expect them to actually find anything they could use against Melchior in his own grimoire. Of course, thinking about it, he has dealt with some tricky and powerful creatures, so he must have had some way to *really* deal with them. "Why don't we freshen up a bit, gather together everything we are going to need, and leave in about an hour?" she suggests.

The others quickly agree to that plan. The sand from the desert is really starting to chafe areas that need no chafing.

Twenty-One

Where was it Again?

Once everyone has cleaned up, they gather all the things they will need and put them in Dirk's magic bag.

"Huh," remarks Tobias. "Did you steal it from Mary Poppins?"

None of the others, however, understand what he is talking about. Dirk is even slightly insulted until Tobias explains that he is talking about a fictional character.

After that, they set off for the rest of their quest. Except Gabriel. Miss Level has explained to him that it's too dangerous for a non-magical person to join them, so, sulkily, he stays home.

Right outside the door, Petulia asks, "Do either of you actually remember where the tree is?"

Miss Level and Dirk gaze in every direction.

"Not really, no," replies Dirk.

"Brilliant start to our quest, wouldn't you say?"

Tobias grabs the stick from his back pocket. "Can we use this to help us find it? It is part of the tree, isn't it?"

"Great idea, young man." Dirk steps closer to him to get a better look, before turning to the other two. "Could we transform it into a locator without alerting Melchior that we are coming?"

"I'm afraid he's known that since I first touched the stick," Petulia remarks. "He just doesn't know how many of us are coming."

"So there wouldn't be any harm in it?"

"I don't think so." Petulia consults her friend. "What do you think?"

"Well, I think it is our best shot." Miss Level turns to Tobias. "Why don't you do the honours? If, by any chance, Melchior *can* actually sense who uses the stick, he won't get any new information about us because you have already used it."

Tobias is thrilled. Miss Level has explained to him how to use magic without spilling it, and he is dying to try it out. "Sure. Just tell me what I need to do."

"All right. It is not that hard. Place the stick lightly in the palms of both hands. Just lying there. That's it. Maybe just a little higher." She waves her hand as an indication for him to raise his. "Perfect. Now, close your eyes and think about the stick you are holding. Feel its weight. Know its length. Now imagine where the stick came from. You can see it as a small branch growing on a tree. It is a dark tree – black, even. Now, gently focus on the whole of the tree. Can you see it?"

Tobias, who appears to be in a sort of trance, nods slowly.

"Great. Now zoom out a little. Can you see the area around the tree?"

Another slow nod.

"Perfect."

The stick in Tobias's hands starts to tremble a little, as if anxious to leave.

"I think the stick misses its tree. Its home. Can you feel it?"

Yet another slow nod.

"Gently close your right hand and hold the stick."

Tobias does as he is told.

"Perfect. Now, assure the stick that you just want to help it get back, and it will lead you there."

There are a few minutes of utter silence while Tobias holds the stick. Suddenly, it points to the east. Slowly, Tobias opens his eyes, sensing that it has worked. "Wow."

Miss Level pats his arm, and Dirk slaps him on the back. All they have to do now is follow the stick. And off they go.

He curses as he stumbles over yet another rock. He is getting tired of this. Tired of walking, tired of stumbling, even tired of turning around and kicking whatever it was that made him stumble in the first place.

Tired in general, he sits down with his back against a tree and puts his head in his hands. Why, oh why did he let himself get captured and be imprisoned in that damn tree? If he had known it would be this hard to find his way again after escaping, he wouldn't have let them put him into the tree in the first place. And unfortunately, he hasn't been able to draw another mural to find out what will happen next.

He sighs and looks up again. The damn tree is standing a few feet away, right in front of him. He has been walking in circles? Seriously? The vilest curse he knows escapes from his lips.

Then, ever so faintly, he feels a flutter of magic pass him by, straight to the tree. Immediately, he rises to his feet and walks over to the tree. There is a definite hum of magic surrounding it. Someone is coming. He places his hands on the bark and tries to sense who it is. A few moments later, he smiles. It's the boy who awoke him in the first place. Perfect. He extracts the smallest scrap of magic from the spell he senses, trying not to alarm the spellcaster, and absorbs it.

If the boy keeps this spell line open, he might be able to find out more about his future visitor, and maybe accumulate enough magic to send him a message.

Twenty-Two

Memories and Loopholes

Tobias feels a gentle tug on the stick. He thinks about asking Miss Level what that might mean, but then decides against it. The tug is gone now, anyway.

Suddenly, he hears the faintest whisper inside his head. Hello, Tobias.

Before he realises what he is doing, he answers in thought. Hello. Who is this?

Wonderful. You can hear me, the silky-smooth voice replies. My name is Melchior.

Immediately, Tobias drops the stick as if it has burned him. The connection is severed. Miss Level, Petulia and Dirk rush to his side.

"What is wrong?" Miss Level asks.

"I heard him," Tobias whispers, his gaze shifting nervously from one person to the next, "in my head."

"Who did you hear?" Miss Level asks, although she already knows what the answer is going to be.

"Melchior."

"Are you sure?" Petulia demands.

"Of course I'm sure," Tobias replies testily. "He introduced himself." As an afterthought, he adds, "He has a nice voice. Very smooth and seductive."

"Damn it." Petulia puts her hands on her hips. "There goes the element of surprise."

Miss Level, however, is more concerned about Tobias. She puts her hand on his arm, trying to soothe him. "Does he know who you are?"

Tobias gulps. "I don't know. He did say my name, though."

Miss Level smiles at him. "It's a good thing you dropped the stick. It severed the connection immediately."

Petulia, meanwhile, realises why Melchior was able to say Tobias's name. "He probably sniffed around inside his head before talking to him. You know that, right?"

"I know," Miss Level replies. "But I also know that Melchior wouldn't have contacted him if he knew we were with him." She gives Tobias's arm another reassuring pat. "You did good."

"You're right." Petulia squints at her friend. "How is that possible?"

Miss Level blushes. "I might have put a blocking spell on Tobias while I was teaching him some tricks." She pats his arm yet again. "I am sorry, dear, but it was for your protection and ours. I should have told you, though."

"Why didn't you?" Tobias asks.

"Well, generally a blocking spell works better when the subject isn't aware of it being cast. When people know it's coming they unconsciously block it."

"But it is all right to tell me now?"

"Oh yes," Miss Level says. "The spell is already cast and working, so it isn't a problem that you are aware of it now."

"So what does that spell do, exactly?" He is a little worried that her tampering with his brain might have some future repercussions.

"Well, it's sort of like putting a veil over certain parts of your memory," Miss Level continues. "Say someone wants to snoop around in your head to find out all sorts of things about you, but you don't want him or her to know something like... I don't know...your cat's name, for instance. Then you put this spell on yourself. And then every time someone snoops around, they won't see anything regarding your cat. No images of you feeding it, playing with it, calling for it. Nothing. As far as they're concerned it's like you don't have a cat at all."

"So you didn't take any of my memories?"

"Oh, heavens, no – if anything, I added some."

"What?"

"Well, Melchior can't see any of us three around you. He also can't see anything you might think about us or say to us. For him, it will appear that you don't know us. But he can see you walking around and stopping and talking to someone. Those someones are just random people. For instance, our conversation right now might appear to him as you asking for directions from a farmer you just met along the way. Do you understand?"

"I think I do, yes."

"Good." She smiles at him. "Now, just one question. Did you get a sense of where the stick was leading us right before you dropped it?"

"Not really, no. It felt like it was just going straight ahead."

"All right, then. Straight ahead it is." Miss Level starts to turn around to continue walking, but then she hesitates a minute. "Should Melchior contact you again, please tell us." At Tobias's startled expression, she quickly adds, "Don't worry, I don't think he will be able to without the connection via the stick, but just in case…" She shrugs. "You might also like to pick up the stick and bring it with you. The spell has been broken so it won't activate again when you pick it up." And then she pivots and continues walking.

Hesitantly, Tobias picks up the stick. Nothing happens. He puts it in his back pocket as usual. Dirk and Petulia look at each other, shrug, and follow.

The connection to the young man has faltered. That is unfortunate.

Did the boy know to whom he was talking, and sever the connection on purpose? That would mean that someone has told the boy about him. Who? And is that person still with him? He didn't sense any companion but he knows well enough that there are easy ways to keep that information from him.

Now he is stuck in this damn forest, near this damn tree in which he was captured for years on end, without any damn magic. He used the bit he absorbed from the spell to talk to Tobias. If only the boy had kept the line open, he could have harvested a bit more magic from him.

As far as he can see, he has two options. Option number one: stay here and wait for the young man to find him. That way, he can use the boy to regain his magical abilities...but he also risks facing whomever is accompanying Tobias. Or option number two: leave and prepare himself for whomever is coming. Most likely, they will try to recapture him.

He sits down, thinks for a bit, and then starts to draw up lists of pros and cons in the sand.

Miss Level is lost in thought. She is fairly certain that Melchior has no idea who is coming, but they may have alarmed him sufficiently for him to go into a defensive mode. She also wonders if he is actually still in the black tree. It is very possible that he has already escaped and isn't anywhere near it. What will they do then? Although he probably has to be in or near the tree to use the locator spell to get in touch with Tobias. She is also surprised that he still has some magic left. Shouldn't it have drained away after years of not using it?

Most people don't realise that magic is a living thing. If you use it, it will be your friend, but if you ignore it, it will go on to the next person who treats it right. It occurs to her that the spilt magic that led them to Tobias in the first place is probably the same magic that Melchior is using. Which also means that he isn't as powerful as he used to be. Most likely, anyway. So unless he's found some other source of magic, they can probably take him down easily enough.

She thinks back, trying to remember where they imprisoned him in the first place. This is not an easy task because, as a precaution, they put a spell on the area surrounding the tree. The people who were there when he was captured have completely forgotten where it occurred. Another feature of the spell is that people who come too close to the tree will be in some way redirected so that they never see it. She wonders if the spell will have any effect on Melchior if he escapes.

Suddenly, she turns to address her companions. "We have completely forgotten about the protection spell around the tree."

It takes a while before Petulia and Dirk understand what Miss Level is talking about. Their eyes widen simultaneously in the moment when they realise what that means. "You are right," they say in unison.

Petulia turns straight to the old man. "You can't be serious, Dirk. Are you actually nervous right now?"

"Slightly." He swallows down his courage.

"What could you possibly be nervous about just now? We are nowhere near the tree." Petulia gestures to the area surrounding them. "And Miss Level is right. The protection spell has probably already sent us in another direction anyway. So what is it?" She realises that she is lashing out at him. But honestly, they kissed and he is ignoring it like it is nothing. Like it is something he dislikes; something to be ignored. Well, he can't ignore her now, can he?

Dirk, who has been fretting about that damn kiss since it happened, is completely blown away by her reaction. How to tell her that it is her he is nervous about? So he just stares at her. Nothing more.

When she realises that even now he will not answer her, she sighs and turns to Miss Level. "Any idea how we can get around the protection spell?"

Miss Level knows well enough that whatever just happened is something that Petulia and Dirk have to sort out for themselves. She will take no part in it. Happy about the change of subject, she replies, "Not really, no." She scratches her head and thinks out loud. "The spell is keeping everyone from going into the area, but it is probably also keeping him from getting out of it. So defusing the spell would mean setting him free. If he has escaped the tree, that is."

"Next time you should build a loophole into a spell like that," Tobias remarks.

Slowly, Miss Level turns to him. "A loophole. A loophole…" She scratches her head again. The others can see the wheels of her mind turning. They know she is close to finding a solution, so they just look at her in silence. "A loophole." Small pause. "A loophole." Suddenly, she smiles. "Of course!" she exclaims. "We can create a loophole now!"

Three frowning faces stare back at her.

"Surely you're supposed to create one when you cast the spell?" Tobias says hesitantly. "How do you expect to create one when the spell has already been cast for I-don't-know-how-many years?"

Miss Level waves away his objections. "No, I don't mean a loophole in that way. I just mean we should create a hole in the circumference of the spell, for just long enough to allow us to pass through."

"I see," Dirk says. "That could actually work."

Petulia chimes in. "That means we still have to find the circumference, though. I bet we haven't even got close to it."

"You're probably right." Miss Level thinks about it for a bit. "There is only one way we are going to find it. Tobias, you lead the way. Just keep walking straight ahead. Petulia, Dirk and I will be following you, holding hands and squinting."

Tobias regards her quizzically. "Squinting?"

"Of course. The only way to see anything, especially a spell, clearly is to blur everything else out. Since Petulia, Dirk and I have the most experience in handling magic, we will most likely pick up on any disturbance."

Petulia and Dirk agree, so they all line up and hold hands before walking on. If anyone were to pass them by, they would marvel at the funny sight. Tobias feels like a kindergarten teacher leading a field trip. But if this is how to find the protection spell, then he won't complain.

He has decided to go for option number two, and is walking away from the tree. This time he is somewhat calmer than before, so the stumbling over roots and rocks is limited. And when it does happen, he refrains from kicking whatever tripped him.

As he walks, he figures that there has to be a reason why he ended up back at the tree. He is certain that he only walked straight ahead. A protection spell would explain it. It would also explain why he can't recognise anything that surrounds him.

Every thirty steps or so he stops walking and looks around, squinting. He can and will figure this out.

Twenty-Three

We're All Geniuses

It had been three days since they'd visited the Academy and learned the horrific truth about Austencia's death. They had decided to split up again and research all the spells they could find. One of them had to work against Melchior. It just had to.

Unfortunately, during those three days, Melchior had not been sitting by in idleness. More and more witches and wizards had disappeared. And what was more, when the missing persons were found again, their power had always been drained and they had been killed. *The Genealogy of Witches* had updated so frequently that Miss Level had locked it away in a cupboard so she didn't have to see it. Besides those gruesome murders, Melchior had also reached the centaur clans. With Alan by his side, all the clans followed him. War was crossing the land and no one could stop it.

"That won't do." Miss Level slapped another book down onto the table.

Petulia, who had been deeply immersed in her own reading, jumped. "What is going on?"

"Oh, I'm sorry." Miss Level sagged in her chair. "It just seems so hopeless. How are we ever going to fight him? He is becoming more and more powerful by the day."

A deep sigh escaped Petulia's lips. "I know." She closed the book in front of her as well. "Nothing like this has ever happened before. That's the problem. We can read about every spell ever cast, but that doesn't help us one bit."

The two women sat together in silence.

After a while, Miss Level rose from her seat. "Maybe some tea will help."

She filled the kettle with water and went through her usual ritual for making tea. This seemed to calm her immensely. When the kettle had whistled and the tea was steeping, she sat back down and stared into her mug. Petulia was right, of course. Nothing like this had ever happened before, so how were they supposed to find a way to fight him? They could read all the books in the world and still not find the answer. Even *The Big Book of Dale* was useless. She lifted the teabag out of her mug. She didn't like tea that was too strong. She never had. Everyone she knew just kept their teabag in their mug. She thought that was weird. She had tried it once but the tea had become so bitter she'd had to chuck it and make a fresh brew... She blinked rapidly. Was that a thought? Was she having a moment of inspiration? Yes, she was. She looked up at Petulia and smiled.

Sensing a weird vibe coming from across the table, Petulia lifted her head and frowned. "Why are you smiling?"

"You are a genius, and I am a genius. We're both geniuses." Miss Level leaped happily from her chair and into the study, returning shortly with parchment and pen. "You are right. Nothing like this has ever happened before, so we can't find any spells we can use. Makes perfect sense." She started babbling. "But that is just it. If we can't find a spell we can use, we can create one." She put the parchment and pen on the table and focused.

Petulia was still a little confused as to why she was suddenly a genius, but she didn't argue. Her friend seemed to be onto something. And in that case, it was best to leave her alone for a while. So, she sipped her tea and watched Miss Level think.

It was starting to become a habit: God's head popped up once a day, just to check if they had found anything yet. That day wasn't any different. "Any progress?" he grumbled by way of greeting.

Petulia rushed over to the bowl on the counter. "Shush," she whispered. "She is thinking."

"What?" he asked loudly.

"I said shush," Petulia countered. "Or do you want me to tip over this bowl?" She glared into the water.

"No," God muttered. "What is she thinking about?"

"A spell." Petulia beamed. Her very own friend was thinking up a powerful spell, and Petulia couldn't have been prouder if she were doing it herself.

"Why?"

"Because there isn't one yet." This made perfect sense to Petulia, but God was having a little more trouble.

"Put me on the table. I want to see."

As requested, Petulia carried the bowl to the table and put it down facing her friend. God's head tilted slightly as he studied

Miss Level. She was sitting with her nose in the air, the pen tapping away against her lip. Occasionally she dropped her eyes to the paper and scribbled furiously; then she scratched away something she'd written earlier and gazed back up. This had been going on for an hour but she was getting closer; she could feel it.

God's head turned around in the bowl. "*Voco* me when she is finished," he whispered. "This looks very promising. And get Dirk there as well." And with those words, his head popped out of the bowl.

Not bothering to put the bowl back on the counter, Petulia sat at the table, crossed her arms, gazing at her friend in wonder. Was that a faint purple glow surrounding her?

Petulia had eventually fallen asleep. It wasn't until Miss Level made a sound that she woke up with a start. In her excitement, Miss Level had pushed her chair back hard, which produced a loud scraping noise before the chair itself crashed to the floor.

"I've got it!" she yelled, dancing around the kitchen. "I think I've really got it!"

Rubbing her eyes, Petulia asked sleepily, "What have you got?"

Miss Level stopped dancing. "I have a spell to fight Melchior."

This immediately roused Petulia. "Really?"

"Yes." Miss Level moved closer to Petulia. "I have thought long and hard about this." She took a deep breath. "With all the power Melchior has absorbed over the last three days, we can't just fight him. It would be a suicide mission. So, I wondered if there might be another way to stop him." A broad smile appeared on her face. "And there is. Or, more accurately, there is *now*."

"All right." Petulia started to feel excited as well. "Explain it to me."

Miss Level sat down and squirmed in her seat. "Well, first we need to get him away from his army. Somewhere secluded." She thought for a bit. "Preferably somewhere with a very big tree or something like that." Shaking her head to clear her thoughts, she looked back at her friend. "When we get him there, we need to keep him there. Probably with a distraction." Another thought. "Or maybe a decoy?" Another shake of her head. "While he is there, we gather around him at a safe distance, so he can't sense us. And then we start chanting!" She stopped talking, watching Petulia closely while smiling at her.

"Uhm…" Petulia felt like she was missing something. "Chanting what, exactly?"

"The spell, of course."

"Right." Petulia waited to see if any other explanation was coming. When it was clear that it was not, she continued, "And what does the spell do?"

Miss Level laughed. "As if you don't know."

"I don't," Petulia replied.

Suddenly, Miss Level stopped laughing, cocked her head, and looked quizzically at Petulia. "You mean I didn't tell you?"

"No – you haven't spoken for about two hours. How could I possibly know what you were thinking?"

"Oh," Miss Level said in surprise. "I guess I must have talked to you in my head. Well, no matter." She patted her friend's hand.

"I have worked out a spell to trap Melchior inside a tree. And to be absolutely sure that no one accidentally wakes him – or, worse, frees him – the spell will also create a barrier around the tree within which nothing will ever be disturbed."

Petulia just stared at her. Lock him up in a tree, with no way for him to be awoken. That was absolute genius. She was very happy to be Miss Level's friend; especially now that she knew what her enemies could encounter. What would it be like to be locked in a tree? Petulia's eyes glazed over as she imagined this.

Not sure what to do about her seemingly frozen friend, Miss Level patted her hand again before rising from her seat. She walked over to the kitchen counter and started to prepare something to eat.

When Petulia finally emerged from her stupor, they *vocoed* God and Dirk. Within half an hour, both men arrived on their doorstep.

Miss Level explained what she had thought up, but with just a little more detail than before. "It is a very powerful spell and will need the help of a few more people."

"How many more do you need?" God grumbled. "What kind of spell cannot be performed by two witches and two wizards?"

"Actually, we need seven people." Miss Level glanced uneasily at the two men on the other side of the table. "More precisely, seven witches."

"What?" God shouted and stood up, leaning forward over the table. "You have *vocoed* us here just to let us know you won't be needing us? This could have been done over a bowl. You know how much I hate to be *vocoed*." His voice rose with every word he uttered.

Dirk cut in. "He is right, you know."

Miss Level had had quite enough of God's blustering. Whenever he'd done it when he was in the bowl she could just ignore it, but now enough was enough. She rose from her seat, giving off a faint purple glow, and said calmly, "Sit down."

God complied immediately, but Miss Level remained standing.

"The spell will draw its power from the five elements, plus two personal elements." Miss Level towered over the men in front of her, which was quite a feat because she really wasn't that tall. "Now, we all know that witches have a greater affinity with the elements than wizards." She squinted at them, daring them to disagree. "And as for the other two elements, one is already a witch." A quick glance in Petulia's direction gave all the explanation that was needed about that. "Adding a wizard to that lot would not only be unwise, it would be dangerous. The flow of the spell would fluctuate and become unstable. So, to complete the circle, the last element will also be represented by a witch." She gazed around the table. "Anyone disagree?"

Three heads shook vigorously.

"Good." Miss Level sank down on her chair, and the purple glow faded away. "Now, we will also need your help. That is why you are here."

"What do you need us to do?" Dirk asked.

Miss Level smiled, knowing that they would not question her again. "First of all, we need five more witches in our little group.

200

I will represent spirit. But we still need water, fire, wind, earth and myrrh. Any thoughts?"

The four companions huddled together and discussed all the options.

Twenty-Four

Preparing the Spell

The first to arrive was Phyllis, which surprised everyone until she opened her mouth. "So, where is the little baby?" she cooed.

Miss Level sighed. "Phyllis, there is no baby." She opened the door a little wider to let the other woman in.

Phyllis walked into the living room and looked around, still absolutely certain that there should be a baby present. When she saw only God, Dirk and Petulia, she turned to Miss Level. "What do you mean, there is no baby?" She frowned, confused. "You did ask me for a baby shower, didn't you?"

"No, Phyllis, I didn't." Miss Level closed the door and joined the others on the sofa. "We asked you here because we need your help."

"Oh, I was sure that it was because of a baby." Phyllis scratched her head. "Oh well, I'm here now. What do you need?" She sat in a chair next to the sofa.

"I am sure you have noticed what is going on in the world," Miss Level began, receiving a grave nod from Phyllis in reply. "And do you know who is behind it?"

An angry glare accompanied the nod this time.

"Good, that helps. Well, we have found a way to stop him, but we need your help, along with that of just a few other witches." Miss Level went on to explain the idea.

With every word spoken, Phyllis's nods became increasingly enthusiastic, until she smiled and applauded. "Bravo! Well done! That is brilliant!"

"So, you will help us?"

"Of course I will."

"And you brought the myrrh?"

Phyllis hit her forehead. "That's it. That is why I thought 'baby'. Last time someone asked me for myrrh, it was to give as a present for a newborn. Although what a newborn could possibly want with myrrh is beyond me." She shook her head.

"Well, that doesn't matter now," Miss Level said quickly, before Phyllis could launch into a speech about myrrh and babies and forget why she was here again. "As you know, Melchior has a real penchant for myrrh. So, we have taken that as one of the personal elements to use against him, and as you grow the stuff in your backyard we believe you would be the perfect witch to represent that element."

"Brilliant, just brilliant." Phyllis shook her head in wonder, and continued to do so for a few minutes.

Becoming a little unnerved by smiling, head-shaking Phyllis, Miss Level stood. "All right, that is settled. Anyone want some tea while we wait for the others?"

"Yes, please," God, Petulia and Dirk said in unison. Apparently, Phyllis was making them nervous as well. God and

Petulia didn't even react to the unison thing. Instead, they all rose from their seats and joined Miss Level in the kitchen, leaving Phyllis alone in the living room.

The next knock on the door brought Gwendolyn into their midst. She didn't need a lot of persuading: Austencia had been her sister. "We didn't always get along, but she didn't deserve that. And to think that he has her power…" She shook her head in anger before staring straight into Miss Level's eyes. "Just tell me what you need me to do."

Before any explanation was given, there came another knock on the door. Opening it, Petulia found Euphagia on the doorstep, in the company of the Briar sisters.

"Right," Miss Level said as the three women joined them. "Now we can get started."

Twenty-Five

Backup

Suddenly, Petulia stops walking, which causes all the others to jerk back and bump into each other.

Miss Level's head collides with Dirk's shoulder. "Ouch!" Letting go of everyone's hand, she rubs hard above her left temple. "This better be good, Petulia."

"I think I can see something." Petulia is squinting at a peculiar-looking rock.

Everyone else turns in the same direction and squints as well. The rock seems to shimmer.

"I believe you might be right," Miss Level says, still rubbing her head. Slowly, she walks over to the rock, squinting of course, because otherwise she would pass it by completely and circle back. When she reaches it, she puts her hand on the rock and feels a zing of power flow through it. She turns and smiles at the others. "We did it. We found the circumference."

They join her, and Petulia puts her hands on her hips. "Now all we have to do is create a hole so that we can get to the other side." She looks at the others. "Any ideas?"

"Not really, no." Miss Level sits down on the ground in front of the rock.

The others follow her example. And there they sit, thinking about how to make a hole in the circumference of a protection spell. It won't be easy. It isn't like the spell Melchior had in his house, where they just had to fiddle with a few magical strings and pick the lock. This is a very powerful spell, created by a bunch of witches to trap an evil wizard. It is a tough one.

The four of them stare at the greenery behind the rock. It doesn't look any different to the rest of the forest. Tobias, who is a little curious about this spell he can't really see, picks up a small rock and throws it, aiming it at the tree a few feet behind the rock by which they are sitting. All of them watch Tobias's rock soar through the air, tumbling over and over. Then all of a sudden it veers sharply to the left and comes rocketing back to him like a boomerang. He catches it and stares at it. The other three do the same thing, throwing rocks and catching them on the rebound. They never really tested the spell that way and are pleasantly surprised that it works. Then they realise that it works really well – too well, actually. How will they ever be able to make a hole in it?

Another ten minutes of fruitless thinking pass by until Dirk suddenly says, "We could send a message to the other witches who helped cast the spell, and ask for their help."

"So you want to tell another five witches that we want to make a hole in the circumference of this brilliant spell because we think Melchior might be awake and on the loose?" Petulia cocks an eyebrow at him. "Do you really think it is a good idea to tell them something like that? What if it turns out to be a false alarm?" The moment those words leave her mouth, she realises that it won't be a false alarm. Tobias heard Melchior's voice in his head.

Dirk sees that realisation clearly on her face. It strengthens him to go against her. "Yes, I *do* think it is a good idea." He points at the young man. "He heard his voice, so Melchior is definitely awake. The only thing we don't know is if he is still in his damn tree." His voice starts to rise. "But if he isn't, I would gladly welcome any help we can get to put him back in it!"

Petulia smiles at him, rattling him just a bit. There he is: the feisty old man she likes arguing with. "You are right. We should send a message."

Miss Level is a bit surprised that Petulia agrees, but she doesn't argue because it is actually a good idea. So she stands up, looks at the sky, and whistles a jaunty tune. A few minutes later, a rather nervous bluebird descends and lands on her outstretched finger. She whistles a few things to the bird. It nods at her and flies away, happy to be leaving this particular spot.

"What did you tell it?" Petulia asks.

"Well, I figured that saying what you said before might indeed alarm them, so I said that the spell needs some reinforcing and that they should meet us here. We will see who shows up." Miss Level sits back down. "And then we will tell them the rest of the story."

Petulia shrugs. "Sounds like a plan. What are we going to do until they show up?"

Tobias chimes in, "Well, to be honest, I am getting quite hungry."

"Good idea, lad," Dirk says. He grabs his bag and starts rummaging through it. Then he pulls out four plates, four glasses, a bottle of wine, bread, and several different kinds of spread and cheese.

They enjoy their meal while pondering the problem before them. Occasionally, one of them looks up, thinking that they have the solution, and then quickly looks down again as they find yet another problem with said solution. Almost the entire meal is consumed in silence. Only the occasional sigh resounds.

About half an hour later, Euphagia appears around the bend in the path. She almost flies right past them on her broom (such a great protection spell). But when Miss Level shouts to her, she immediately turns around and joins them. She greets everyone warmly (even Tobias, whom she has never met before), then sits down and helps herself to some cheese. A few minutes after that, Gwendolyn whooshes by and then stops abruptly a few feet away from them. She had her broom on cruise control while squinting at her surroundings, so she saw the five of them sitting near the rock. She too joins their little party. The next to arrive, about an hour later, is Phyllis. She is on foot because her broom is in the shop for maintenance. She waves at them from afar. As she is short-sighted, for her simply taking off her glasses is as good as squinting. Next are the Briar sisters. They are natural witches, and because they are twins their connection makes them even more powerful. They ride in on a two-seater broom.

"Is that my broom?" Miss Level stands up. She really doesn't like the sisters. They always steal stuff, even though they are more than powerful enough to make it for themselves.

"It looks like it," Petulia replies. "You should have taken out a patent." She hates the sisters too, mostly because she dislikes anyone with natural powers, except Miss Level.

Dirk grumbles, "That means they were in my office without me there." He dislikes them because they think they are better than everyone else – which of course they are, but they don't have to flaunt it – and because they have no respect for other people or their personal belongings.

The sisters fly up to them. "So what is the emergency?"

"Did you not listen to the message I sent?" Miss Level is flustered.

"We only listen to the first sentence of any message we receive," says Esme.

"It saves us a bunch of time because people always repeat the rest of the message when you see them anyway," finishes Viola.

"So," Esme repeats, "what is the emergency?"

Actually, Euphagia, Gwendolyn and Phyllis are wondering the same thing. They found it strange that this spell needs renewing, but curiosity got the better of them and so they came. Now all five of the new companions cross their arms and wait.

"Well," Miss Level starts, "we believe that Melchior has awakened and that he might escape."

The five witches glance at each other in surprise.

Sensing that they don't quite understand the severity of the situation, Petulia adds, "He might actually have escaped already, but he should be stuck inside the circumference of the spell."

"So we are here to reinforce the spell," Esme says, "and make sure he can't get out."

"Actually, we had a different plan." Miss Level turns to Tobias. "Come here."

Tobias rises and moves closer to Miss Level, who puts her arm around his waist – she can't reach his shoulders – and introduces him. "This is Tobias. He only recently came into our world."

"Did you make another man?" Viola walks around them. "I don't see a tail or horns, so you must have done something right."

"Ha ha ha," Petulia says sarcastically.

Miss Level tries to keep calm. "No, we did not create him. He came here by himself."

Intrigued, Viola waves her hand. "Continue."

Rolling her eyes internally, Miss Level does as she is told. "He opened a portal. With this." She nudges Tobias, who reaches into his back pocket, pulls out the black stick and shows it to all of them.

At once the five witches suck in a breath and take a step back. "How is that possible?" they say in unison. Then ten eyes swivel to Dirk, who just shrugs.

"Exactly," Petulia replies. "And that is what we intend to find out."

Miss Level clears her throat. "Also, we found Melchior's place of residence and acquired his grimoire."

"No!" Ten eyes widen.

"Yes!" Miss Level starts to get carried away with her enthusiasm. "We were even able to look into it, and may have found a way to destroy Melchior."

The five new companions gape at the others in astonishment. None of them expected anything like that.

Esme is the first to speak. "So what do you need us for?"

"Well, we need to get in there but we don't want to break down the spell."

Esme laughs. "That isn't possible, anyway!"

Petulia narrows her eyes at the Briar sister, silently warning her not to laugh again. "We thought it might be possible to make a hole in the circumference – one just big enough to let us in."

Viola scratches her chin. Hesitantly, she says, "That might be possible. Hang on a minute." She closes her eyes and raises her head, as if looking at the sky. Deep in thought, she occasionally murmurs a few words to herself. Suddenly, her eyes open wide and she smiles. "Eureka!"

Squinting, he looks around. Suddenly, his eyes are drawn to a fern. It looks as if squiggly lines are coming from it. He steps closer, still squinting. There is definitely something there. With every step closer, he is more certain that the fern is surrounded by magic.

When he reaches the fern, he gets down on his haunches and touches it. A zing of power shoots up his fingertips and through his arm. "That is some grade-A type of magic." He absorbs some of the residual power and flushes. He isn't nearly as powerful as he used to be, but every little bit helps. He touches the fern again and is rewarded with another zing of power. "This is the life."

Then he sits down, feeling very tired of walking, and lets his fingers run over the fern leaves. His head lolls back as he starts to relax.

Twenty-Six

Opening a Window

"We can use the stick!" Viola exclaims.

"What?" Petulia is confused. "How?"

"Yes," Euphagia says, "do please explain."

Viola sits down, and the rest of them follow her example. "The stick is part of the tree, right?"

"Right," they all say, in unison, although everyone is getting really tired of that.

"And the tree is part of the spell, isn't it?"

A bit hesitant, but still in unison. "It is."

"I believe that if we use the stick to draw a circle in the invisible wall of the circumference, it might just create a portal-like window."

"Not quite the eureka-worthy thing I was expecting." Esme is not impressed. "Still, it might work."

Viola looks around at the group. "So who wants to draw a circle?"

"Well, Tobias has always been the one to wield the stick, so I think he should do the honours." Miss Level smiles reassuringly at him.

Tobias glances nervously around and sees ten witchy eyes gazing at him, weighing and measuring him, and finding him wanting.

"Are you sure about that?" Gwendolyn asks.

Even Euphagia, who is the most positive person in the group, has her doubts.

"Yes," Miss Level says firmly, brooking no further questioning of her intuition, "I am sure."

Tobias wishes he felt as confident as her, but he really does want to help, so he says, "I am new to magic, but if any of you can tell me exactly what to do, then I am sure I can do it."

This does not instil confidence in the others. Esme and Viola roll their eyes simultaneously.

Esme holds out her hand. "Just give the stick to me and I will do it."

"No!" exclaims Miss Level. "And I will give you two reasons why not. First of all, Tobias really can pull this off. He has more natural power than any of you believe he has. And secondly, so far he has been the only one to wield the stick. Do you understand? He is the *only one*."

Quizzical frowns and stares meet her pointed gaze.

She rolls her eyes. "Melchior knows only that Tobias is coming. He might have an inkling that someone is with him, but he has no idea who or how many of us. If any of you touches the stick, you can be damn sure he will know that it is us, and he will prepare accordingly."

Esme is impressed with that logic but refuses to acknowledge it. "If he is even awake."

Miss Level shoots her a murderous look. Already she is seriously regretting sending a message to the twins. "He is awake. And he knows about Tobias. He even talked to him through the connection of the stick."

"You never mentioned that." Viola springs up. "I am out of here. He has probably heard every word we've said!"

Petulia stands up and puts her hands on her hips. "Sit down, Viola," she says sternly. "He hasn't heard any of this. We severed the connection." Realising that they need to get back on track, she adds, "Well, actually, Tobias did. With his quick thinking." She winks at him, and he smiles back at her. Maybe she isn't such a grumpy old witch.

Tobias can see fresh respect in a few of the witches' eyes, although Esme and Viola are not yet convinced. He directs himself straight at the twins and says firmly, "I can do this. Just tell me what it is I need to do."

"Fine." Esme rises as well. "Come here. It's very easy."

Tobias joins her next to the rock.

"If you squint your eyes, you can see the squiggly lines of the circumference of the spell. Can you see them?"

Tobias almost tells her that he isn't that much of a newbie, but swallows his words just in time. "Yes."

"Hang on." Esme turns to the others. "Are we all going, or are some of us staying behind?"

"Good question." Dirk has been silent for so long that everyone almost forgot that he's here – or everyone except Petulia, of course. Somehow, she can sense him without even wanting to. It's very annoying. "I believe the hole in the circumference will close again, will it not?"

Esme just nods.

"Then I would suggest we all go in," Dirk decides. "It will give us more power in case Melchior has in fact escaped the tree so that we can put him back inside it. And if the hole doesn't close completely, someone can stay near it on the inside, just in case he tries to escape."

"Fine." Esme turns back to the invisible wall. "Then we should make the hole big enough, because it will start closing up the minute it is fully drawn." She nudges Tobias. "Go ahead. Grab the stick and hold it like a pen."

He does as he is told.

"Now reach up as far as you can, even go on your tiptoes, and then plunge the stick straight into the wall."

Tobias hesitates, mostly because he can't see a wall, and because he has the feeling that he will just topple over into the shrubs.

Miss Level realises where his hesitation is coming from. "Tobias," she says.

He turns to her, standing on his toes with his arm raised high.

"Don't worry. You will feel a resistance. Like a force field. You won't fall over." She smiles.

He turns back to the invisible wall, closes his eyes, and plunges the stick forward. She is right!

216

Quickly, Esme continues, "Now make a circle all the way to the bottom, just above the ground, and then back up again, closing the circle."

Slowly, Tobias draws the circle. The spell offers a lot of resistance but he is able to mark out and close the circle within five minutes. A small flash appears, and the middle of the circle vanishes. Nobody has to squint to see the edge shimmer and slowly start to close. Everyone grabs their stuff and slips through the opening. Dirk doesn't bother to collect up the leftover picnic food. He only takes his bag and follows. Right behind him, the circle closes. Everyone has made it through.

Still sitting with his eyes closed, he gently strokes the fern again. All of a sudden, a jolt of amazing power runs through him, filling him from head to toe.

"Wow!" His eyes snap open. That was a big hit of raw power. What happened? And more importantly, who caused it? Has the boy found him?

He touches the fern again. It is still buzzing with magic but the level has gone back down to what it was. So the protection spell is still intact. His shoulders sag. He shouldn't have got his hopes up. The boy probably doesn't have enough power to break the spell.

"I will just stay here with you, then," he sighs, and goes back to stroking the fern.

Twenty-Seven

And... Action

It was ghostly quiet in the forest. It seemed like all the animals knew something was going to happen and had scurried off to their hiding places.

Only two minutes ago, Miss Level had seen Melchior racing down the path on his broom. She had pretended to be picking herbs, minding her own business. But the moment he'd rounded the corner, she had taken her own broom, which had been hidden behind a nearby tree, and set off to her designated spot.

Dirk was already waiting there. "Did you see him?"

"Yes," Miss Level said as she jumped from her broom. "He whizzed by, not paying any attention to me or anything else."

"I guess that's good, right?" Dirk lifted his bag and rummaged through it.

"I hope so, but it also means we don't have much time." She stretched out her hand towards him, just as he lifted a small parcel from his bag. "Thank you." Immediately, she started to open it. "Now, go to the next in line and help her prepare."

Without another word, Dirk mounted his broom and zipped off.

Everything had been prepared down to the last detail. God had lured Melchior to a specific spot in the forest, right next to a very big, very old oak tree. Around this tree, at a distance sufficient not to be sensed by Melchior, the witches had drawn a circumference. Miss Level had been on the lookout for Melchior so that they'd know when they needed to close the circle and begin the spell. Now Dirk and his bottomless bag went counterclockwise around the circle, handing everyone their supplies and signalling to them to get ready. Each witch would receive an ever-lighting candle, a prepared herb pouch, and one thing specific to the element she would represent.

The first in line was Gwendolyn, who would be representing water. As soon as Dirk came into view, she stepped onto her marked spot and opened her hand. Dirk didn't say a word. He didn't even step down from his broom; he just grabbed the right parcel out of his bag and handed it to her before flying away. From it she retrieved a vial of water along with the other supplies. This water had been taken from the cave in which Melchior's home was located, to ensure a personal connection with him. The second witch to receive a parcel was Phyllis. She would represent one of the personal elements for Melchior: myrrh. Next was Esme, one of the Briar sisters, who had a close affinity with earth. Her parcel included a vial of sand from Melchior's cave. Euphagia, representing fire, came after that. The extra part of her parcel was also a vial. This one had been tricky. Miss Level had retrieved it, along with the other elements, from Melchior's cave.

On entering the castle she had taken a burning torch from his hallway, picked a small flame from it, and dropped it into the vial before it extinguished, keeping it magically aflame.

The fifth witch in the circle was Petulia. She received an empty vial in her parcel. As Dirk sped away from her, she opened it, pulled out a few strands of her hair, and put them in the vial. She was the second of the personal elements establishing a link with Melchior: herself. Before Miss Level had explained the spell to the rest of them, Petulia had told her that she would have to tell them about her history with Melchior. She had dreaded it, but knew that it had to be done. The looks the others had given her had been awful. They had been furious with her, as she had known they would be. But she had raised her head, taken their insults, and assured them that she wanted the same thing they did: to stop Melchior from doing any more harm. They had grumbled and muttered, but eventually had accepted Miss Level's word that Petulia was needed if the spell were to succeed. So here she was, making damn sure that they *would* succeed.

The sixth witch – Viola, the other Briar sister – represented air and received a seemingly empty vial. It was, however, filled with air from Melchior's cave.

By the time Dirk returned to Miss Level, who was the next and last person in the circle, each of the witches was standing ready with her candle and vial in her left hand and her herb pouch in her right. Miss Level's vial had been the hardest to fill. To best represent spirit, she had returned to Austencia's body and pressed on the dead woman's chest to force her last breath from her lungs, capturing that wisp of spirit in her own vial. It had been dreadful to be back in that place but she'd known it had to be done. And now she was as ready as the rest of them. Miss Level nodded to Dirk. He cupped his hands over his mouth and hooted like an owl.

In the middle of the circle, God had welcomed Melchior and thanked him for coming.

"Yes, of course." Melchior smiled, standing face to face with him. "Why wouldn't I come?" His red eyes were ghastly.

If God had had any doubts that Melchior had gone dark, they vanished at the sight of those eyes. He swallowed down the lump in his throat. Why had he agreed to do this? Right. Evil man. He smiled back at Melchior. "Well, it has been a while since we last spoke." He fidgeted with the cuff of his shirtsleeve. "I have heard about all the things you have been up to and I wanted to congratulate you."

One of Melchior's eyebrows lifted in a perfect arch. "Congratulate me?"

"Of course." God laughed and walked over to the other man's side, slapping him on the back. "I remember the conversation we had about bending people to your will and all, and I just wanted to congratulate you on how well it has worked. You know." He laughed again, but a little more nervously than before.

Melchior narrowed his eyes and cocked his head slightly. For a few moments, he just stared at God in silence, sizing him up. Finally, he spoke. "So, why did you want to meet here?"

God walked over to his other side. "Well, I know that most people don't understand you. That they, you know, hate you for what you have been doing. But I just wanted to let you know that *I* don't, you know, hate you. I think you're doing a swell job, and I wanted to offer my services. No need to force me, you know." A humourless laugh escaped him. He swallowed again.

Melchior stepped closer to him and whispered, "But I like it."

"Ha, well, who wouldn't?" God shrugged in an attempt to look relaxed. It didn't work.

And then an owl hooted.

At the sound of the hoot, Miss Level held her pouch of herbs above her candle flame. The moment it ignited, she dropped the candle to the ground where it was immediately extinguished, not being held upright any more. She lifted her left hand, in which the vial of Austencia's spirit lay flat on her palm. Holding the burning herbs in her right hand, she drew circles around the hand with the vial, all the while chanting the spell she had written. She knew the others were doing the exact same thing at the exact same time.

The vial lifted slightly from Miss Level's hand. Suddenly, a purple beam of energy burst from it and swept through the forest towards Gwendolyn. It hit the vial in Gwendolyn's palm, heating it up a little, before it lifted as well. Another burst of energy escaped from the other side of the vial. This time, it was blue. The blue line of energy entered Phyllis's vial and exited coloured terracotta brown. In Esme's vial, it became green. Euphagia's representation of fire turned the line red. When it connected with Petulia's vial, it started to shake violently. Petulia inhaled deeply before continuing to chant, focusing all her energy on the vial in her hand and willing it not to drop. Then it lifted, and a bright white line burst out of it. Viola's vial transformed the energy for the last time, giving it a warm yellow colour before it raced back towards its starting point in Miss Level's vial.

The circle was complete, creating a colourful circumference around the tree. Slowly, the line widened, spreading upwards in a multicoloured veil that rose and formed a dome over the tree that was standing right in its middle.

The second he heard the owl hoot, God knew that his time was up. Unfortunately, that was also the moment when Melchior realised that he was being set up.

And Melchior was faster. At once he threw a freeze spell at God. "So." He stepped even closer to him, absolutely certain that there wasn't a thing he could do. "You lured me here to do what exactly?" Circling God, he continued, "You must have realised that I would figure it out." He cocked his head. "So does that make you collateral damage, or just stupid?"

God could do nothing. Every inch of him was frozen in its last position. Fortunately, he had just been standing at that point. He had been frozen in much worse positions. If he could have, he would have shuddered at the memory. But as it was, he could do nothing but think; he couldn't even blink. Good thing the mind is the most powerful weapon. Over and over, he recited these words in his mind: I don't want to be frozen. I don't want to be frozen. I don't want to be frozen.

As he was repeating this one sentence, Melchior kept talking to him. "Are you alone, or are there other people out here, waiting for your signal or something?" He glanced around but couldn't see anything out of the ordinary. "How cowardly of them to keep their distance." He looked back at God. "I do admire your courage." He circled back around to face the frozen man in front of him and smiled. "I am going to love bending you to my will, especially after your little attempt before."

And then the smile faded from Melchior's face. Had God just blinked? He stared at him. It couldn't be. Still slightly frozen, God looked up with just his eyes. Melchior couldn't resist following his gaze. Almost directly above them, a multicoloured veil was on the cusp of closing over them. Melchior's jaw dropped. The moment the veil closed, a heavy string of energy raced down towards the ground. It hit the tree next to them and seemed to drain all the colour from it.

"Miss me," Melchior said, still gazing at the tree.

God didn't hesitate. He pushed Melchior as hard as he could towards the now-blackened tree. In reflex, Melchior turned to see God run away from him. Furious, he prepared to cast the most awful spell he knew. It had worked well on Austencia, and it would work well on God.

He made just one mistake: he wasn't looking at the tree any more. Several branches whipped around, grabbing him firmly. A surprised yelp escaped him. He struggled with all his might but could not get free. The branches dragged him towards the trunk. He watched in horror as the bark opened up, revealing a dark hole just big enough for one man. In desperation, he snapped off a twig from the tree and focused all his energy on it before throwing it away from him like a spear. Then he gave himself up to the tree, hoping with all his might that the little stick would find its way back to him. When it did, his revenge would be great. The bark closed around him, as if tucking him into bed, and he fell into a dreamless sleep.

Miss Level saw the veil creeping nearer to the ground. The spell was almost complete. From within the circumference she heard footsteps getting closer and closer, accompanied by very loud breathing.

Suddenly, God rolled across the ground next to her, barely escaping Melchior's last desperate assault. Only a second later, the veil reached the ground and snapped shut, creating an impenetrable dome around the tree. The colours faded, and an invisible barrier was all that remained. God lay panting. He had never run so fast in his life, and he would never do it again. He would make damn sure of it.

Miss Level sank down next to him. "Did it work?" she asked hesitantly.

All God could do was nod.

"Good." She lay down next to him, resting.

After a few moments they could hear the soft whoosh of brooms drawing near. The others joined them, and likewise stretched out on the ground. It had been a very powerful spell, and a very draining one. It would be some time before they were at full power again, but it had been worth it.

Dirk opened his bag, lifted out a few bottles of wine and some glasses, and passed them around. Within minutes everyone was sitting upright, drinking, thinking, and most importantly smiling and laughing.

It was at that moment that the Witches' Guild was born. And who better to lead it than the man supplying them with wine?

Twenty-Eight

A Whole Tree

They stand still, right inside the circumference of the spell. This space doesn't look much different to the rest of the forest; maybe a bit more overgrown.

"It looks…" Euphagia pauses to think of the right word, "fuller than I remember."

"I know what you mean," says Gwendolyn. "There are shrubs and ferns everywhere. How can that be?"

Esme rolls her eyes. "Because no people or animals were allowed in here. That is why." She starts to walk away from the invisible wall, which is intact once more. "Also, it has been hundreds of years since we were last here. Things are bound to have changed a bit."

"Do you even know where you are going?" Petulia asks.

"It doesn't matter," Esme replies. "The protection spell will make us end up at the tree, so we can just start walking in any direction."

Miss Level shrugs at Petulia and follows. Everyone else does likewise, so Petulia joins them.

Euphagia shivers. "It is quite disturbing how quiet it is in here. No birds singing or animals scurrying around." She shivers again. "Eerie."

"Maybe we should refrain from talking," Petulia remarks. "If he *is* out, he might hear us coming."

"That actually sounds like a good idea." Esme is surprised that it was Petulia who came up with it.

Petulia just shrugs. She doesn't like talking to these people and now she has a good excuse. Inwardly, she smiles. Miss Level, of course, knows exactly why Petulia suggested this, but her professed explanation has some logic so she just rolls her eyes and continues walking.

It doesn't take them too long to find the tree. Esme was right: they are inexplicably drawn to it. Well, maybe not inexplicably for them, but for anybody else it would seem weird. At first sight, the tree seems just as they left it, but when they surround it they find a gaping hole in its bark.

"Damn it." Petulia puts her hands on her hips; her standard pose for when she is annoyed.

"My sentiments exactly." Esme mimics her.

Euphagia, Gwendolyn and Phyllis stare open-mouthed at the tree. Somehow they haven't wanted to believe that Melchior escaping was an actual possibility. Now, being confronted with that outcome has left them bewildered. Had they known this had happened, they would never have crossed the threshold of the spell. 'Damn it' doesn't quite cover it for them.

Viola and Miss Level are already pondering their next move. They look around cautiously. Is Melchior watching them right now? If so, what is his plan? How powerful is he? He probably isn't *that* powerful, otherwise he would have attacked them already. He is a smite-now-ask-questions-later kind of guy. But it won't take him long to come up with something. He must have sensed their entrance…or hasn't he? In any case, they will need to come up with a defensive strategy, so they should prepare.

Tobias and Dirk stare at the tree as well. What would it be like to be stuck inside a tree for that long? There doesn't seem to be a lot of legroom. What did Melchior do when he had to pee? Simultaneously, both men lean forward.

Suddenly, Tobias feels the stick in his back pocket vibrate. Before he has a chance to grab it, it flies out and slams into the tree, merging immediately with the bark. It almost sounds like it lets out the tiniest of sighs, happy to be back. The tree begins to shake. The blackness fades from it and seeps into the ground, leaving an old but healthy-looking oak behind. Even the gaping hole in the trunk simply closes up.

In silence the companions watch the transformation, not quite knowing what to do. Miss Level is the first to move. Slowly, she walks over to the tree and puts her hand on the trunk. Immediately, her gaze snaps upwards and a purple glow starts to spread through her. The others take a step back. It is never easy to determine what is happening in a situation like this. Is Miss Level absorbing the power of the tree, or is it Melchior's power that is running through her right now?

After a full five minutes, she slowly returns her head to its normal position and withdraws her hand. "I wondered if that would happen."

"Well, it did," Petulia chimes in. "Are you happy? You are now chock-a-block full of Melchior's power. Again."

"Again?!" The others raise their voices in question, and in unison.

Petulia flutters her hand as if to wave away their objections. She looks at Miss Level. "Well? What do you have to say for yourself?"

Miss Level just smiles. "Nothing." She is still glowing with a faint purple hue. "Just that I don't think Melchior has a lot of power right now." She gazes at the spot where the stick has merged with the rest of the tree. "I think he was waiting for that stick to return. He put all his power in it before the tree sealed him in, and now that power is back." She turns back to her companions. "And I have it."

He hears a noise. It is coming from where the tree is.

Suddenly, he remembers the stick and springs to his feet, running in the general direction of the tree. Any direction is good enough, anyway. He doesn't even realise that he is stumbling along.

As abruptly as he started running, he stops again. If he actually did hear a noise, that would mean that whoever is in here with him heard it too, or caused it. What is the best course of action? Running headlong into the fray doesn't seem like such a good idea any more. He needs to know what has happened.

As stealthily as he possibly can, he moves slowly forward.

Twenty-Nine

Making a Plan

Usually, everybody likes Miss Level. She is a very likeable person. But right now, with that weird grin on her face, everyone fears her a little. They know that she is a good person and a good witch, without an evil bone in her body. But with Melchior's power running through her, will she remain that way? Miss Level herself is not scared. Why would she be? But for the first time since meeting her, Petulia is scared for her friend.

Rummaging in his bag, Dirk steps up to Miss Level. This is fascinating. He would be a fool not to take advantage of it. "Excuse me, Miss Level, but may I do a few tests on you?"

"What kind of tests?"

"Oh, just taking your temperature, listening to your heartbeat, things like that."

She doesn't see the harm in that, so she nods her consent. He pulls a thermometer out of his bag and sticks it in her mouth. Next, he takes a stethoscope and somewhat hesitantly places it against her chest. To be honest, he has never been this close to a woman's bosom before, so his hand shakes a little. He doesn't hear anything out of the ordinary. He takes the thermometer out of her mouth and gazes at it. Normal body temperature.

His hand goes back into the bag and pulls out a tiny looking glass with a light on it. "Say, 'Aaaah.'"

She does as she's told.

Looking into her mouth, he again notices nothing unusual. He moves to her side and puts the apparatus in her ear. "Aha!" Inside her ear, he can still see a subtle purple glow. He has no idea what that means, of course, but he is glad that he has found something.

Petulia comes over, takes the looking glass out of his hand, and looks into her friend's ear herself. She notices the purple glow as well. "What do you mean, 'Aha'? It's just some residual glow. That happens all the time."

Dirk cocks his eyebrow at her. "It does?"

"Yes." She hands him back his looking glass. "Purple is the natural colour of Miss Level's magic. Every time her magic builds up, she turns purple." She waves her hand. "It is nothing to be worried about. As long as it's purple, we are good to go."

Dirk looks again at Miss Level, who just shrugs and says, "She's right."

He turns to the rest of the group. They all shrug too.

Annoyed at not having discovered anything at all, he shoves the looking glass back into his bag. "Fine."

Tobias feels a bit sorry for him. So when Dirk comes back to stand next to him, he slaps him reassuringly on the back. "I was impressed."

Dirk huffs. "Great. I impressed a layman." Sarcasm does not become him, but right now he does not care.

Tobias, feeling a bit offended, takes back his hand and shoves it into his pocket.

By this time, Gwendolyn, Euphagia and Phyllis have digested all the information about the tree, the tree curing itself, Miss Level glowing, and her having all the power of Melchior. This causes three things to happen: Gwendolyn faints, Phyllis throws up, and Euphagia starts to laugh uncontrollably. A firm slap to her face from Esme manages to snap her out of that.

Then Esme turns back, rubbing her hand. That slap might have been just a tad too hard. "We need a plan." She sits down on the ground. When nobody follows her example, she looks up at them and says, "Look, if Melchior attacks us and we don't have a plan, we are sitting ducks anyway. We might as well sit down for a minute and think before we go running off to do who knows what."

"You are right." Viola sits down next to her sister. "Let us take a minute and think."

Petulia turns to Dirk. "Do you by any chance have some more wine in that bag of yours? To help with the thinking." She smiles at him, hoping that this will bring him out of his sulk.

He appreciates the gesture, and sticks his hand back into his bag. Glasses and two bottles of wine are passed around. But before you judge them for drinking on the job, here is something you probably did not know: witches do not get drunk, and especially not on wine. Some spirits might do the trick, but they do not like the taste of them. However, wine (especially a nice

Cabernet Franc) has a taste they think is heavenly, and instead of clouding their minds, it lifts their spirits and makes them think more clearly.

Before long the ideas start coming. Then suddenly Viola exclaims, "Wait a minute. Didn't you say you found something in Melchior's grimoire that might do the trick?"

"You are right." Miss Level holds out her hands to Dirk, who reluctantly lifts the grimoire out of his bag.

"You brought that *here*?" Esme is astounded that they have done such a stupid thing. "What if he gets his hands on it?"

"Relax," replies Miss Level. "We sort of hacked it. If he finds it and opens it, all he will see is a bunch of gibberish."

"How did you manage that?" Esme narrows her eyes at Miss Level. "You used *The Big Book of Dale*, didn't you?"

"Of course we did." Petulia butts in. "If you had a book like that, wouldn't *you* use it?" She shakes her head. "What a stupid question."

Miss Level opens the grimoire. "Now, where was it?" She turns the pages for a good ten minutes – it is a very thick book – until she finds the right passage. "Ah, here it is."

She hands the open book to Esme. Immediately, Viola, Euphagia, Gwendolyn and Phyllis lean in to read with her.

"You are right. That ought to do the trick."

Phyllis frowns. "I don't understand."

"Of course you don't." Petulia looks closely at her. "Are you even wearing the right glasses?"

Slightly offended, Phyllis replies, "Yes, I am", and then pushes her glasses further up her nose.

Petulia raises her hands in surrender. "All right, then, what is it you don't understand?"

"When do we use the squirrel?"

"In the middle bit."

"And where do we get it? There are no animals in here."

Petulia has to admit that, actually, that is a very good question. She looks around at the others. They have come to the same conclusion.

"Huh," is the only response given.

He has almost reached the tree. Slowly, he creeps up to the last tree that stands between him and the black one, and presses his back to the trunk. He can hear voices, but can't make out what they are saying. Slowly, he peeks out from behind the tree, trying to be as inconspicuous as possible. There they are: the people responsible for putting him in that damn tree. The boy is with them as well. It looks like they are having a tea party right in front of the damn thing.

Suddenly, he notices that the tree is no longer black and that the gaping hole in its trunk has vanished. How is that possible? Of course – the stick. Does that mean that his power has returned to the tree? He looks at the witches in front of it. And if it has, is that power still in there?

He needs to get closer without drawing any attention to himself. He gets down on his hands and knees and starts to crawl in a circle around the tree. Can he reach the other side, where they aren't looking, without them noticing him? So far, so good.

Thirty

Ducks and Squirrels

Dirk has an idea. He has never tried it before, but he can't see any reason why he can't just pull a squirrel out of his bag. In theory, the bag holds anything his heart desires, and right now, that is a squirrel. Slowly, he slips his left hand into the bag, concentrating intensely on finding a squirrel in there. After a while, his entire arm has disappeared into the bag.

Miss Level is the first to see what he is doing, and quickly realises what he is trying to accomplish. After that, it is Petulia who notices the curious look on Miss Level's face. Following her friend's gaze, she sees Dirk's look of concentration and just as quickly realises what is going on. She nudges Esme with her elbow, and in turn Esme nudges Viola. The nudge is passed on until everyone within their little circle is looking at Dirk and holding their breath.

Suddenly, the concentration on Dirk's face turns into joy. He removes his arm from the bag and triumphantly holds up…a rabbit. He frowns at it. "I was sure I had caught a squirrel."

"Clearly, you haven't," Petulia replies. "Can I give it a try?"

To her surprise, he hands over his bag to her. "Sure. Go ahead." Then he puts the rabbit on his lap and strokes it, while watching her thrust her hand into the bag.

Petulia feels around. Why does he keep these things in here? A basketball, a baseball bat, a hockey stick, a pot of flowers, several glasses, plates, and pieces of silverware. Well, the last few she understands as she has already used some of those items. She shakes her head and tries to concentrate. Squirrel, squirrel, squirrel. When her hand brushes something furry, she grabs it and pulls it out. A badger. A little disappointed, she releases the animal into the shrubbery, and it immediately scuttles off.

Esme takes the bag from her. "Let me try." Her hand also disappears, but she feels nothing; just the lining of the bag. She frowns, concentrates, and tries again. Without any success.

Viola is next. Like her sister before her, she can feel only the lining of the bag. "I don't understand. Why can't we find anything?"

A little annoyed, Dirk replies, "Maybe because you didn't ask permission? You just grabbed the bag and delved in. The bag senses my feelings, and he won't let you use him because *I* won't let you use him."

Esme rolls her eyes. "That is stupid and selfish of you. We just want to help."

"Well, help in another way." Dirk crosses his arms.

Tobias figures he might try it as well. "Can I?"

"Of course you can, young man." Dirk gestures to Viola to hand over the bag to Tobias.

Reluctantly, she does so.

"Manners are very important," Dirk mumbles.

Slowly, Tobias lowers his right hand into the bag. At first, he can't feel a thing. Then he figures that the bag is probably like the stick from Melchior's tree: if he focuses on what he wants, it might magically appear. He closes his eyes and thinks about forest animals. Then he zooms in on those animals that live in trees. After that, he zooms in a little more on animals that live in trees but aren't birds. After a while, he has a clear picture of a squirrel hopping from one branch to the next. He focuses and grabs it. When he lifts his hand from the bag there is indeed a squirrel struggling to be released. Tobias looks around triumphantly and smiles. Miss Level applauds, smiling right back at him. Esme and Viola try to look uninterested but are secretly envious. Petulia shrugs. She knows she has a concentration problem; that's why so many of her spells backfire. Usually, halfway through them, she gets distracted by something or other. Dirk is very pleased as well. He noticed that the young man has great potential, and he is always happy when one of his senses is actually accurate.

All of a sudden, from within a nearby bush they hear a twig snap. Nine heads spin in the direction of the sound. Each one of them is as quiet as a mouse.

A minute passes before Phyllis whispers, "Do you think it is him?"

A beat later Esme answers, "No. And if it was him, that means he hasn't got any power. Otherwise, he would have attacked right away. We are pretty much sitting ducks here."

It takes another five minutes before the badger trudges back out of the shrubs and rejoins them. A general sigh of relief is exhaled by all.

That was close. The moment his knee hit the twig, he scrunched his face and hoped they hadn't heard. But judging by the silence that greeted him, he knew immediately that that was wishful thinking. Please don't come over here. Please don't come over here, he prayed silently. And then he heard a little scuttle from within a nearby bush. A badger poked its head out, and immediately he grabbed the creature and thrust it in the direction of the witches.

When he hears their sigh of relief, he exhales. Just to be sure, he waits a few more minutes before continuing his crawl. He is almost there. He raises his head to see if anyone is still looking this way. No one. Trying to be as stealthy as possible, he tumbles over to a rock that sits near the tree. No one seems to notice. He actually starts to wonder what they are doing. But not for too long.

With another roll he ends up beside the tree in which he spent so many years. He feels a little resentful of it, but right now he just wants his power back. Ever so slowly and carefully, he puts out his hands, closes his eyes and touches the trunk.

Nothing. Damn it. They already have his power. Of course, they are just sitting around and eating cake, or whatever it is they are eating. He bows his head. Now what?

Tobias notices some movement behind the tree. Did he just hear a sigh as well? Without attracting too much attention, he leans over to the right-hand side of the tree, trying to look around it, but it really is a big-ass tree. It should be: a man was stuck in there for several years.

Of course, Miss Level, being the watchful type, sees how oddly Tobias is behaving. She cocks her head, trying to figure out what he is doing. When she realises, she straightens her back, readying herself for the imminent attack. But none comes. She frowns and turns to the tree.

"What—" Petulia starts, but her friend shushes her. Sensing that it might have something to do with Melchior, Petulia follows Miss Level's instruction.

The others have finally realised something going on as well. They hear the shushing and decide to do the same.

Slowly, Miss Level rises from her seat on the ground.

It has become very quiet on the other side of the tree. Too quiet. He tenses, ready for anything. Oh, who is he kidding? He isn't ready for anything at all. His shoulders sag and he just waits.

Miss Level creeps around the tree. A defeated old man seems to be waiting for her.

"Melchior?" She is astonished at the sight of this once-powerful man. He looks so harmless.

He raises his head. "Miss Level." He greets her politely with a little nod. "Just do whatever it is you came here to do."

By this time, the others have followed her around the tree. This is him? Tobias thinks. This is the great Melchior? He looks like an old man, bent over in supplication. Tobias expected someone broad and tall, exuding charisma. There are nine of them against this one shrivelled man. How disappointing. Petulia feels almost the same, except for the fact that she knew Melchior at the height of his power. Did his time in the tree really reduce him to this? She feels sorry for him, and for being one of the people who put him there. In this state, he isn't a threat any more. He is just someone they should take care of. Esme and Viola aren't sure what to think. This man is nothing: a waste of space, and a waste of their precious time. But is he like this because he had a change of heart, or because he has been without power for so long? They can easily let the others handle this, but what if Melchior's feebleness is just a facade? Gwendolyn and Phyllis don't think anything at all. They are waiting for someone to say something, and then they will just go along with whatever has been decided.

Euphagia cocks her head. "You don't have any power, do you?" She is a firm believer in asking the question to which you want to know the answer. Guessing is a waste of time, so she doesn't do it.

To everyone's surprise, Melchior bursts into tears. Wow – they would never have expected that. Attack, yes. Cunning move, yes. Defence, even, yes. But breaking down in front of them, never, no way.

Petulia feels slightly guilty. If it wasn't for her, Melchior might still be a wonderful and good wizard. Maybe if she had said yes when he proposed to her she could have prevented him from turning evil and kept him from that dark path. But she soon realises that his decline was not her fault. He was already on that path when he proposed, and somehow she knows she still wouldn't have accepted him even if he hadn't gone all red-eyed.

She casts a sideways glance at Dirk. He is looking at her intently. Of course, he knows all about her history with Melchior. Then again, who doesn't? What is he thinking now?

Dirk, in turn, wants to know the same thing about Petulia. What is she thinking? Has seeing Melchior again rekindled her feelings? Will she go back to him? And then without any warning, Dirk thinks, Do I still have a shot with her? That thought comes out of nowhere. He is completely blown away, and embarrassed. He glances away.

Is Petulia misreading the look Dirk just gave her? No time to dwell on that. She needs to make sure Miss Level stays away from Melchior. Her friend has always had a soft spot for the weak. As Petulia is thinking that, she sees Miss Level's face contort in empathy for the man at her feet. Immediately, Petulia jumps forward and slaps away Miss Level's outstretched hands. "Don't touch him."

This startles Miss Level. "What are you doing?"

"I just don't trust him." Petulia looks down at Melchior. "What if he is just acting?"

Nine heads, cocked sideways, turn to the snivelling figure on the ground.

Esme is the first to speak. "I don't see it."

Melchior wipes his nose on his sleeve.

"I *really* don't see it," Esme reiterates.

"I don't care," Petulia says. "Even if it is not a game or a con or whatever," she turns to Miss Level, "you are not touching him."

He genuinely was not acting. He felt miserable and just wanted it over with – whatever they planned to do to him.

But now he starts to regain some of his hope. There is a reason Petulia doesn't want Miss Level to touch him, and he is pretty sure he knows exactly what it is.

Thirty-One

Binding

"But look at him." Miss Level pouts. "He looks so...so forlorn."

"I don't care." Petulia wedges herself between her friend and the man on the ground. "You are not going anywhere near him." She looks down at Melchior in disgust. "If he needs a hug, he can get it somewhere else."

"Fine." Miss Level steps back and crosses her arms. "Any ideas for what to do next?"

"What do you mean?"

"Well, I am not inclined to use the spell we had in mind on him. I mean, look at him." Miss Level gestures at Melchior, although she does notice that the frequency of his snivels has reduced somewhat. "But we have to do something, right? We can't just leave him here."

"She makes a good point," Esme chimes in.

Petulia takes a deep breath. "Fine. Now, let me think." She crosses one arm in front of her and taps her chin with her other hand.

Phyllis decides to join the conversation. "We could bind his powers and take him with us?"

Despite the fact that this is a suggestion from Phyllis, it is actually a very good one.

Or so it seems, until Euphagia says, "I thought he didn't have any powers?" Frowning, she looks around at the rest of the group. "How can we bind something that isn't there?"

"I am pretty sure that he still has some power left," Petulia says. "He would not be caught dead without any." She looks at Phyllis. "All right. I like that idea. Let's do it."

By this time, Melchior's snivelling has stopped completely. Miss Level has been watching him for a few minutes, and saw the calculated look that appeared in his eyes. Petulia is right. He will never stop being the evil creature they locked into the tree. Miss Level needs to intervene before the others begin the binding ritual. She has the distinct impression that he will be able to draw power from that small spell. Not a lot, but enough to do something. Vaguely, she hears Phyllis tell everyone that she will look for rope. Gwendolyn, wanting to be useful too, says she will make the puppet. Miss Level glances at Dirk, who is about to remind everyone that he has a magic bag. But when he sees the look on her face and the tiny shake of her head, he snaps his mouth shut. He knows better than to doubt Miss Level. If she has a plan, he will follow it to the letter.

Esme and Viola have decided that nothing eventful is happening and that it won't happen for a while, so they return to the other side of the tree and continue drinking their wine. They will chat about nonsensical things until a better pastime reveals itself.

Euphagia joins Petulia. Both women look down at Melchior. "So, do you really think a binding could work?"

Petulia grabs Euphagia's arm and pulls her away from the tree. "No. I don't think it will work, but I do think she," motioning to Miss Level, who is standing a bit further away, "will come up with something. But for that to happen, the others had to leave." She looks Euphagia right in the eye. "Can you help us?"

"Sure." Euphagia shrugs. "What do you need me to do?"

"I need you to make sure the others don't come back. Also, get the sisters to move away from the tree." Petulia lets go of Euphagia's arm and waits for a response.

None comes. Euphagia just turns around and walks over to the sisters. Petulia can't hear what she is saying to them, but the result is very satisfying. Reluctantly, Esme and Viola stand up and walk away with her.

All this time, Tobias watches everyone doing what they are doing. He doesn't quite understand what is going on. Are they doing the binding or not? Just to be safe, he will stand here and wait. He glances to his left. It looks like Dirk is taking exactly the same approach.

There is a lot of activity going on, and most of it is concentrated somewhere away from him. Cautiously, he lifts his head. Miss Level is standing right there. He can reach out his hand and touch her.

Ever so slowly, he lifts his right hand and inches it forward. He tries to keep his breathing steady, which is quite hard because he is very excited. He is only twelve inches away from regaining some of his power! Slowly. Slow…ly! Just one more inch away from her foot. He walks his fingers over the ground.

And then she moves her foot!

Miss Level cocks her head and looks down at the hopeful man in front of her. "Did you really think I didn't notice what you were doing?" She smiles. "Have your brains deserted you as well as your power?" She can see the resentment in his eyes as he looks up at her.

"Fine." He grits his teeth. "Have it your way."

All of a sudden, he springs to his feet and lunges at her. She dodges like a pro. This, of course, makes him furious; so furious that he casts a small spell at her that sends her stumbling to the ground. She crawls away backwards, still able to escape his clutches. He casts another small spell, freezing her in position. With a grin, he walks slowly over to her.

Tobias and Dirk aren't just going to stand by and do nothing. As one they leap forward and grab Melchior, making sure that none of their bare flesh touches his, which will allow him to steal some of their power. He growls at them, demanding that they let him go.

He knows he doesn't have that many options left. He can see the other witches hurrying back towards them. There is only one thing left to do. He casts his final spell, sending them all toppling over each other. That drains the last of his power. Freed, he turns to Miss Level, who is still frozen on the ground. He runs to her, reaching for her. So close!

And then she blinks. He stops dead in his tracks, thinking only two things: How can that be? and, Not again!

The confusion is plainly visible on Melchior's face, right up until Petulia smacks him on the head with the heaviest branch she could find. Immediately, he crumples to the ground, unconscious.

"Well, that took you long enough." Miss Level twitches her fingers, trying to get the life back into the rest of her body. "Is he drained?"

"Completely." Petulia lifts Melchior's limp hand. "That last spell was the end of it."

"I knew he wouldn't be able to resist."

The others stand back up and draw near.

Esme is the first to speak. "I figured you had a plan." Really, she didn't, but she'll never admit that to anyone. "Good choice of branch, Petulia. But, Miss Level, how did you escape the freezing spell?"

Miss Level shrugs, mostly to shake the last of the freezing spell out of her shoulders. "It is a little trick I picked up from God. I figured Melchior might try to freeze me because he did the same to God when we first gathered here."

"So what happens next?" Gwendolyn asks nervously. She doesn't like the sight of the sprawled figure on the ground.

"I say we bind him with actual rope," Miss Level says. "And we make sure no magic can ever get close to him, ever again."

Tobias grins and says, "I know just the place to put him."

Thirty-Two

A Fitting End

The tent flap moves, although there is not a breeze around. Elizabella nudges Adelbert, who has fallen asleep on the cushions.

"What?" he asks sleepily, and yawns.

"I think they are back," she whispers.

This, of course, has the same rousing effect as ten cups of ristretto. Adelbert jumps to his feet.

The flap opens, and in walk Tobias and Petulia.

Petulia clears her throat. "I know that last time we didn't part in the best of circumstances—"

"Not the best of circumstances?" Adelbert interrupts. "You disappeared, leaving Elizabella distraught, and I am quite certain that your little…*thing* in the ruin is what caused the last mural to crack as well." His face turns bright red.

Unperturbed, Petulia finishes, "…but we come bearing gifts."

At that moment, Dirk pushes the tied-up Melchior through the opening of the tent. Elizabella and Adelbert gape at him, unable to utter a single word.

"If you promise to care for and worship him, as we all know you want to, we will leave him here."

The couple nod vigorously.

"There are just two conditions." Petulia puts on her sternest face ever. "You cannot tell other people about this, and you cannot let him out of your sight – ever." She wags her finger at them. "Not. Ever. Do you understand?"

Another bout of vigorous nods.

Petulia steps up to them and holds up her hands. "Pinkie swear."

Pinkies are linked and shaken. Petulia smiles. Stupid people – they don't know how powerful a pinkie swear is. If they break it, she will know immediately. And it is the only spell that cannot be drained. She is certain that Melchior is in good hands here. Who knows? He might even enjoy himself.

She turns to Tobias. "Let's go."

Tobias says a polite goodbye to Elizabella and Adelbert. Then he looks at Melchior. It is a shame they didn't meet when he was still good and powerful. Tobias could have learned a lot from him. Oh, well. He is also sure that he can learn a lot at the Witches' Guild, and the Head Master was thrilled when he told him he'll be back. Life will be good. Tobias is certain of it.

A final wave and off they go; far enough away that Melchior doesn't receive any residual magic.

www.ingramcontent.com/pod-product-compliance
Lightning Source LLC
Chambersburg PA
CBHW031121030726
47496CB00002BA/640